ABOUT THE AUTHOR

Matthew Yorke is the author of *The March Fence* (Winner of the John Llewellyn Rhys Prize), *Chancing It* and *Pictures of Lily* (Shortlisted for Not the Booker Prize). He also edited *Surviving: The Uncollected Writings of Henry Green*. *Fish Tale* is his fourth novel. He lives in London.

Fish Tale

Matthew Yorke

COGITO Publishing
Published by COGITO Publishing Limited,
4/4a Bloomsbury Square, London WC1A 2RP

COGITO Publishing Limited, Registered Office:
4/4a Bloomsbury Square, London WC1A 2RP, England

www.cogitopublishing.co.uk

Typeset in Sabon MT by
Palimpsest Book Production Ltd, Falkirk, Stirlingshire

Printed and bound in Great Britain by Clays Ltd, Elcograf S.p.A.

A CIP catalogue record for this book
is available from the British Library

ISBN: 978-1-9196053-3-3

COGITO Publishing is committed to a sustainable future for our business, our readers and our planet. This book is made from papers made from responsible sources.

www.cogitopublishing.co.uk

To Rose B

Fish Tale

Nick Winter

The period leading up to the royal family's arrival at Balmoral for the summer vacation was always a time of great stress for Nick Winter, head ghillie on the castle's four beats of the River Dee. Would the royal party enjoy good fishing? Or wouldn't they?

"You're to stop this fretting, Nick," would be his wife's continual refrain as the day approached. "What use can come from worry? Tell me that?"

"But what if they don't catch fish, Angela?"

"That'll not be your fault!"

"What happens if there aren't any fish?"

"Not your fault again!"

Angela was right. The Dee wasn't the only river to suffer a decline in salmon numbers over the past half-century. And this in spite of efforts to prevent too many fish from being netted at the mouth of the river at Aberdeen; and targets to apprehend poachers, in places like Aboyne and Potarch, being well exceeded. Yet still fewer and fewer fish were caught on the castle's beats. Some said it was down to pollution; others blamed disease.

In truth there was very little Nick could do. It would take a brave man to poach fish from the castle's water, so night patrols with a lamp were for the most part uneventful. His main jobs, then, were control of the redds, the salmon's spawning grounds, and upkeep of the riverbanks, shoring them up in areas where they had been spate-damaged. As well as more mundane tasks: maintenance of the piers from which members of the royal family and their guests actually stood when angling, for instance. Could the boards take the weight of a seventeen-stone man? Were they adequately covered in chicken wire, which would prevent anyone from slipping in wet weather?

• • •

In moments of stress like this Nick might be visited in his dreams by a lady in white, whom he called Freya. Nothing would ever actually be consummated in these dreams; nevertheless they had definite erotic undertones. Freya would be by an open window, a breeze billowing a gossamer-thin gown. Through it you could see the shape of her breasts, which to the touch would be of untold softness.

Nick welcomed these encounters. Freya seemed to be telling him that in the grand scheme of things all his worries were but naught. That when the final *Day of Judgment* came it wouldn't matter a fig whether or not the royal party caught a fish. Indeed, waking from a dream of Freya, his only thought: What an extraordinary apparition this nymph in white. How reassuring to have finally encountered something so real!

His only regret was that Freya wasn't a complete

stranger. The fact was there was a picture of her at the castle. Not inside the castle proper, but outside the rod room door, which was situated close to the servants' entrance. In the picture Freya was standing by a window, her head thrown back as she smiled into a starry sky. Her hair was long, way down below her waist, but not so arranged as to obscure her legs and hips, which were pearly-white and clearly visible through her veil-like gown. The picture, Pre-Raphaelite in style, was framed in black lacquered wood and was about the size of an extra-large letterbox stood on end.

An inscription on a white band held by two nails, read: *UNTIL WE MEET AGAIN.*

• • •

Of course Nick never spoke of Freya to his wife, although Angela may well have suspected he met someone in his sleep, as sometimes he would awake from his dreams very aroused. In truth she welcomed this someone, as she enjoyed making love.

"Another hard Winter," she would whisper playfully in his ear.

• • •

The day of reckoning finally came.

The royal party had arrived by train four days previously, and later that morning Nick was to meet the King and a guest at *Otter's Hole*, the pool the King always opened the season with. There had been some heavy rain during the week, with reports of fish moving through the system.

And Freya had visited, too. In fact Nick had awoken with a glow that seemed to emanate from the very core of his being.

"There, now," Angela said to him, handing him his piece box at the door, "see how you are a different man when the time comes."

"I know," he had to quietly concede.

"Cometh the hour, cometh the man."

• • •

Nick reached *Otter's Hole* well ahead of the royal party. The water might have been the colour of beer, but if the rain held off it would fine down well during the course of the day, he knew from experience. In fact fishing conditions looked decidedly promising. First he baled out the boat and fixed the rowlocks. Then he swept the pier as thoroughly as he might sweep his own sitting room floor, pushing off any detritus into the boiling water.

Presently the King arrived. He was wearing a green tweed suit and a rust-coloured tie. He was smiling broadly, as he enjoyed his fishing.

"Good morning, Nick," he said, shaking his ghillie warmly by the hand.

"Good morning, Sir."

"I'll fish from the boat to start with, and Lord Embers

will fish from the bank. Then we'll swap over at lunch. What do you think about that?"

The King always spoke in this way, which was meant to put his staff at ease.

"Very good, Your Majesty," Nick replied.

Nick doffed his cap to Lord Embers and shook him lightly by the hand. Lord Embers was the King's private secretary, and Nick had ghillied for him on many occasions in the past. He was a heavy man with heavy features. And quite often when it was his turn in the boat he would curse as he tried to find his feet on the swell. But only, of course, when well out of earshot of the King.

Once Nick had loaded the boat with the Sovereign's tackle and once he was sure that Lord Embers was not in need of any further assistance, he helped the King embark. Then they set off towards an island of sun-whitened stone.

"So, Nick, how are you?" the King asked him.

"Very well, Sir."

"And Mrs. Winter?"

"She's well, too, Sir."

"I'm afraid everyone seems a little out of sorts in London at present."

"You've not been poorly, I trust?"

"Oh good heavens no, I've been champion," the King stressed. "Only," he paused before continuing: "Tell me, Nick, do you have any godchildren?"

"I do, Sir."

"And how many, may I ask?"

"I have two goddaughters, Sir."

"Very nice, too. But do you know how many godchildren I've got?"

And when Nick didn't ask, the King told him:

"Sixteen! Did you hear that, Nick? *Sixteen*!"

"That's quite a number, Sir."

"And still counting!"

"That *is* quite a number, Sir," Nick repeated.

"But how to stop people asking? And how to decline? Those are the questions," the King sighed.

• • •

All morning they fished the swim on the lee side of the island and had drawn a blank. Until a few minutes before lunch the King hooked a small grilse. Nick had seen many fish taken at this place, where, like a seal's snout, a boulder broke the surface of the water, so it was no surprise to him to see the Sovereign's line tighten.

"We're in!" the King shouted.

It was an enormous relief to Nick that the King had hooked a fish, and as he kept the boat steady against the current, he found himself praying to Freya. "Don't let the fish get away . . . please, Freya!"

She didn't; and after what turned out to be a lively contest the grilse was in the boat, its spade-like tail slapping the boards beneath the King's feet. The Sovereign always dispatched his own fish, which he accomplished with a silver priest.

"What a beauty!" he marvelled.

• • •

Lord Embers had caught a fish, too, slightly larger than the King's.

"Well done, Embers," Nick heard the King congratulate him as they made their way towards the fishing hut, where lunch awaited them.

• • •

Lacking any kind of finesse, Lord Embers would never rise a fish in the stiller water, the boat rocking in the way it did every time he cast his line; and so, after lunch, Nick took the King's private secretary out to a pool above the island, where there was some faster water.

"Tell me, Winter," he said, as they made their way back up to the top of the pool to start a second drift, "are you a godfather?"

"I am, sir," Nick replied.

"And how many godchildren do you have?"

"Two, sir."

"Genders?"

"I have two goddaughters, sir."

"And you have children yourself, don't you, Winter?"

"Two sons, sir."

"And do they have godparents?"

"Indeed they do, sir."

"And how did you choose them, if I may ask?"

"Well, sir, my wife chose one and I chose the other."

"Very sensible."

• • •

"So how did you get on?" Angela asked Nick when he reached home that night.

"Two fish in *Otter's Hole*," was the reply.

"Two fish in *Otter's Hole*! Well, isn't that just grand! And doesn't that just go to show?"

"Show what?" Nick pretended not to understand.

"To trust," was the reply, said in all seriousness.

Nick took Angela in his arms. Her face was round, her crossbow lips perfectly formed. He kissed her, not full on the mouth, but slightly to one side, where he had learnt over time he could taste her better. He stared into her eyes, deep wells of peat.

"And the King was in good spirits?" Angela asked him.

"A rotten temper," Nick grimaced.

"How so?"

"You know Embers?"

"The private secretary, you mean?"

"I reckon he's asked the King to be godfather to one of his children."

• • •

The following morning something unexpected happened.

The beat the King and Lord Embers were going to fish later that day was higher up the valley, and for this reason, as was the custom, Nick was to meet the party at the castle before travelling on. He had arrived early and had been in and out of the rod room twice, loading tackle into the royal Land Rover, when he became increasingly aware that something wasn't "quite right". At first he thought it must have been the scent from a vase of lilies that was standing on a table next to the hallway's stone fireplace, as never before had he seen flowers in these parts. Until he realized, the blood running cold in his veins, that the picture of Freya was missing.

It would be no use asking Mrs. Fellowes, whom he could see at the head of the corridor organizing fresh linen for the day and who had ideas above her station, anyway; but Big Ben, the King's valet, might know.

"Big Ben, what's happened to the picture that was hanging over there?" he asked, taking the valet by the elbow to lead him down the narrow passageway.

"You mean Veronica?"

"Veronica?" Nick repeated, doing his best to stifle the tone of affront in his voice.

"The woman who was hanging here, you mean? The woman in white?"

"Why do you call her Veronica?"

And when Big Ben couldn't come up with an answer, Nick pressed him.

"But where is she, Big Ben? Where's the picture?"

"Lord Embers had it taken away."

"Lord *Embers* had it taken away?"

"He said it was pornographic and it might offend the King if ever he came down here."

"The King's often down here," Nick retorted.

"That's all I know, Nick," Big Ben shrugged.

"So where's the picture now?"

"That I couldn't tell you."

"But who actually took it down?"

"As far as I know Morton came with the pickup."

• • •

That morning the King fished from the bank, and it was Lord Embers who was in the boat first. Nick was astounded by his strength of feeling. With every cast he loathed him the more, this overweight, arrogant man, with his stentorian breathing and brilliantine hair. What would be the future now that Freya was gone, Nick couldn't stop asking himself. Would he ever dream of her again? And if not, did that mean that the days were gone now, too, of waking with that fuller sensation in his groin?

All of a sudden everything seemed desperately precarious. He might have had a nervous disposition and a tendency to worry, but this was nothing compared to the thought of losing Freya. She was, after all, the balm to the fear that drove these preoccupations of dread, the gatekeeper of that glow of wholeness, the glow that seemed to emanate from the very essence of his being.

Then, out of the blue, Lord Embers hooked a fish.

"I'm in, Winter!" he shouted, his voice so loud it came booming back from the wall of rock in front of them.

"Take me to him . . . Come on, man, look sharp!"

If it were the King's salmon they would have played it from where they were situated, in a relatively quiet patch of water, just on the edge of the riffle. But Lord Embers had different ideas, possibly because he felt there was a better chance of landing his fish by following it downstream. So Nick did what he was told and edged the boat into the neck of the pool. Only the swell here was greater than he thought, and one pull of the oars and they were driven broadside down through the white water.

It wasn't Nick's fault that Lord Embers was suddenly facing the wrong way, although Lord Embers wasn't generous or clear-headed enough to acknowledge this – quite the opposite, in fact.

"You bloody man! I'm warning you . . . if we lose this fish . . ."

No sooner were the words out of his mouth than the line went slack.

"And I ***HAVE*** lost it as well . . . you bloody man," Lord Embers shouted.

"I'm sorry, Milord," Nick shouted back, doing his best to control the boat.

"You ***BER-LUDDDY*** fool!"

Nick could take no more of this. Releasing his hold on the oars, where they swung violently in the rowlocks, he placed both hands on either side of the boat and gave it one great heave. Such a violent heave, in fact, that the craft nearly capsized.

The last he saw of Lord Embers before he went over was the soles of his waders, a sort of waxy-yellow colour.

• • •

It had all happened so quickly that for a moment Nick was frozen by shock and indecision. His first idea was to jump in after Lord Embers, although this wouldn't have been of much use, as already His Lordship was some distance downstream – almost fifty metres, in fact. The best bet would be to row to shore, beach the boat and run down the riverbank to below a point where he thought Lord Embers might end up, and then wade in to collar him.

This, in principle, was a sound plan; the only trouble being the river was still in part spate – it had rained heavily in the night – and Lord Embers was travelling too fast. Which meant that by the time Nick had raced to the bottom of the pool, Lord Embers was already in the white water of the pool below. To reach the tail end of this pool, Nick had to scale a fence and head inland to circumvent some withies. And by the time he had returned to the pebbly shores of the Dee there was no sign of Lord Embers at all. Convinced that he couldn't have "outrun" him, so to speak, Nick began to walk upstream. To a point where he found his charge "hanked", as they say in Scotland, by a tree that had fallen across the top of the pool.

His Lordship was clearly dead, as the current here was strong, too strong to allow the poor man to keep his head above the waves.

• • •

That night as Nick lay next to Angela he was once more amazed by his feelings – or lack of them, this time. Basically he had murdered Lord Embers. How was it he felt no remorse, no guilt?

Of course he hadn't told the police he'd murdered the King's private secretary. He had just described the moment of excitement when Lord Embers had hooked a fish and the confusion that had followed. In fact the detective – who was a keen angler himself – had had a definite shine in his eye as he asked Nick:

"Do you mean to say that Lord Embers wasn't good in the boat?"

"How can I put it, he was a little heavy, sir," Nick had answered.

• • •

The King in his generosity was anxious to put Nick's mind at ease, too. He came down in person to visit the following morning. Quite often the King had been in Nick and Angela's small sitting room – the King was like that: not only was he familiar with his employees, he liked to see for himself the conditions in which they lived – he even had his "own chair".

"You mustn't blame yourself even for one moment," he began. "These accidents happen so dreadfully quickly."

And Nick found himself able to answer without any compunction: "We shouldn't have strayed into the white water, Sir."

"But Lord Embers was determined you did! And therein lies the tragedy. In fact it's probably more my fault than yours. And I'll tell you why. Embers and I had taken a wager about who would catch the first fish of the day. He was probably trying to bank his winnings, so to speak."

"It's good of you to say so, Sir."

"You must have off as much time as you need to get over this most unfortunate incident," the King went on.

"If you don't mind, Sir, I'd like to return to my duties as soon as possible."

"You would?"

"It wouldn't do to just sit here, Your Majesty."

"You're a good man," the King nodded, which later on, when Nick thought back to the conversation, made him feel more than a little awkward.

• • •

The question was what to do about Freya? Although, in reality, what could be done?

That night Nick dreamt of her again. The tone of the dream wasn't so different, a little diluted perhaps. But unquestionably Freya's demeanour was changed. Not that he could really see. Whereas in his previous dreams she would be standing as she was in the picture at the castle, her head thrown back, her gossamer gown trailing from her shoulders, this time she was seated before an open window, her back to him as with one hand she supported her chin, elbow on knee. Her flesh was the same pearly-white colour and her hair that chestnut-brown. But this time, when he awoke, Nick found he wasn't hard.

Was that on account of guilt? he asked himself. Would that be his punishment, known only to himself? Impotence?

• • •

Early the following morning, which was a Sunday, Nick went to find Morton, foreman of Balmoral's tradesmen. He was a small, wiry man with a canny manner.

"A picture, Winter? Which picture?"

"It was entitled *UNTIL WE MEET AGAIN*."

"I've no recollection of it."

"But you must!" Nick betrayed himself.

"And what if I did?" Morton asked him, slyly. "What if I did take charge of this picture?"

"I would like to have the opportunity of . . . of obtaining it," Nick answered him.

"That may not be so easy," Morton told him.

"Won't you see what you can do?"

And he tipped the rogue £10, the same £10 that Lord Embers had tipped Nick at the conclusion of fishing on that first day when his Lordship had caught a fish, his last fish it was to turn out.

Constancia Acosta

Never having had any children of his own, the King's sixteen godchildren were, in fact, a blessing to him. His favourite of all was called Constancia Acosta. The daughter of a polo-playing friend, she was unusually beautiful, with long, flowing auburn hair and glowing skin, freckled like an apricot.

Constancia had been raised in Buenos Aires, where her childhood had been idyllic: she had literally wanted for nothing. And like a lot of young women when they reach the age of eighteen she had discovered a love of travel. The flight from Rio de Janeiro to Paris – her preferred route into Europe – she always liked to undertake at night, when in the darkened cabin of an aircraft she could imagine the miles of empty ocean below.

• • •

It was fun for Constancia to be the King of England's goddaughter. She had plenty of friends in Europe, but if ever she felt she needed something different she had only to pick up the phone. It didn't matter where the King was, he would always ask her to stay – and to bring a friend, too, if she so pleased.

"I'm coming to the UK next week," she informed him from her hotel room in Lima, where that summer she was breaking her journey to meet some friends.

"Then you must come and stay," was the King's response.

"Where will you be?"

"In Scotland. We are here for the duration of the holidays. Why don't you bring a friend? It will stop you from being bored."

"You know I am never bored when I am in your company," Constancia laughed. "Perhaps if you are in Scotland I could go fishing?" she mused, remembering how much she had enjoyed her days on the river there, the stillness of the man into whose care she had been placed, and the success she had enjoyed on that occasion, too – a brace of fresh-run salmon, lilac-silver and deep bellied – when the other members of the royal party had drawn a blank.

"Of course you may fish! The season has started rather better than we expected. Only we had a tragedy," the King added, his voice a little strained.

"You did?"

"A man was drowned on the river, a member of my staff."

"I'm so sorry."

"He wasn't wearing his life vest. If he had, things may have been different."

• • •

Constancia had broken her journey in Peru in order to visit friends who lived in the jungle outside Iquitos. These friends were the proprietors of a healing centre, where a curandero – a shaman or native healer – would perform ceremonies for locals and tourists passing through.

On the night of her arrival, she drank a cup of the shaman's medicine and had the strangest vision. She dreamt she was on the banks of the King's river in Scotland accompanied by Nick Winter, the quiet man in whose care she had been entrusted. She had hooked a fish in a pool called *Brigadier's Elbow*, and had played it with great skill and patience. All had been well until the moment Nick stood and bent to scoop the bar of silver into the boat with the royal net. As soon as it touched the bare boards it turned into a whippet.

"My god, Winter, what have we here?" she cried. "I can't possibly kill this."

"We must return it from where it came," Nick said with quiet conviction; and holding the whippet by the scruff of its neck, he lowered it carefully back into the peaty water.

Where it reverted to its previous form, a freshly run salmon.

• • •

The following morning, with the help of her friends, Constancia tried to fathom what this dream could have meant. One of them thought it was a warning. "Didn't the King tell you someone had drowned on the river?" he said. "Your spirit is urging you to be vigilant." Another thought the vision advised exploring more obvious aspects within herself. Symbols didn't come much more potent than rivers and dogs, she insisted. And in the dream neither had appeared menacing, had they?

"Not in the least," Constancia told them.

There was one man there who had made the pilgrimage to the Amazon from Oregon to overcome his obsession with gambling.

"I agree with the first speaker: I think you should take great care," he said with a grave expression. "If I had had that dream I would be worried."

Constancia laughed him off. "You foolish man! What have I to be worried about?"

"All I'm saying is I think you should be careful."

"Well, thank you for your generosity of spirit," she laughed again.

• • •

Secretly she admired this man, however, as there was something about his troubled frown and ebony eyes that she found deeply attractive.

"Do you know the King of England?" she asked him later on that morning.

"I don't believe I do," was the lazy reply.

"Would you care to visit him in Scotland? I am going there next week and he has suggested I bring a friend.

Otherwise he thinks I may get bored," she added with a coquettish smile.

"Let me think about it," the man said.

• • •

Naturally this stranger from Oregon, whose name was Kai Nelson, was curious to visit the King of England.

On leaving the healing centre, he travelled to Lima with Constancia, where she was to fly to Paris and he was booked on a plane to London. They stayed the night in a hotel in Miraflores, ate ceviche from oval-shaped plates and drank piscos, then made love overlooking the Pacific.

"Do you think you will come with me to Balmoral?" Constancia asked him.

"I don't see why not," he replied.

Kai

When he reached London, Kai went straight to a meeting of *Gamblers Anonymous.* Not because he felt any compulsion to gamble, but because he wished to spread the word about his cure.

"I have just come back from the rainforest in Peru," he said when it was his turn to speak, "and I feel something has changed within me. This was brought about by a series of ceremonies in which I drank some medicine and encountered various spirits, who thankfully have lifted this obligation I seem to be under to take risks."

After the meeting a man called Cal introduced himself to Kai.

"I'm curious to know more about your experiences in South America. How did it work?" he asked him.

"I've no idea how it worked," Kai replied. "I was staying in the jungle where the advice was not to venture off the path into the bush: to do so you would almost certainly have got lost. I had to face my demons, and one by one they fell away."

"You do not believe in the spiritual side of our programme, then?" Cal asked him.

"Most certainly I do, but I have touched on something more fundamental, I sense."

And when Cal continued to look doubtful, Kai tried to explain further.

"It goes without saying that man cannot live by bread alone. That to lead a sober and meaningful life we must submit to a Higher Authority, always endeavouring to exist not in isolation, but in harmony with our fellow man. Yet this conviction alone has never been sufficient to lift my compulsion to act rashly. That is what I have addressed in the jungle."

• • •

The following morning Kai met Constancia at Heathrow airport and together they flew on to Aberdeen. The King was delighted to see them both. He had never been to northern California, so he was especially interested to meet Kai.

"You have trees there that are a thousand years old, I hear."

"We do, Sir."

"And one that you can actually drive through," the King laughed.

"That tree may no longer exist," Kai informed him. "I believe it came down in a gale."

"Well, we have gales here, too," the King nodded, sagely. "Now, let us go and see your quarters. I always like to go in person with my guests to make sure they are comfortable when they stay with me."

So following Big Ben, who, owing to his build and strength, was able to carry all of Constancia's and Kai's luggage, they climbed the stone staircase to the top floor.

"Naturally you may sleep wherever you like," the King said, showing them two adjoining rooms, but indicating the long corridor that stretched like a vein through a mine of rock. "Explore the castle, make yourself at home."

"Thank you, dear godfather," Constancia said, squeezing his hand.

"Thank you, Sir," Kai bowed.

• • •

Kai may have thought he was free of his compulsion to gamble, but later that afternoon, after he and Constancia had made love in front of a window with views on to a forest of pine, his resolve was put to the test.

The King liked to have as many distractions as possible, and beyond the French windows of the library there was a small putting green.

"Let's have a shot or two," he suggested to Kai.

"I would like that," Kai replied.

Once they had the weight of the clubs and the feel of the green, the King then said: "A sovereign I sink this next putt."

"Sir, I never wager," Kai objected.

"Nonsense," the King declaimed, and took his shot, which thankfully missed. "There you are," he said, pulling a gold sovereign from his pocket and pressing it into his guest's palm.

"But I never wager," Kai insisted.

"A fine fellow you'll be if you don't allow me to win it back!" the King protested, lining up his next shot.

By the end of the evening Kai had five golden sovereigns in his pocket.

• • •

The next morning they went fishing. Kai was no stranger to the art of angling and preferred to fish from the bank. There was room for two to fish from the boat, so the King and Constancia went out with Nick Winter.

"You remember Nick, don't you, Constancia?" the King said at their introduction.

"I remember him well," Constancia replied.

At lunch Kai had caught two small grilse to the King's and Constancia's single kelt, an ugly, red fish, which they had returned to the water.

So Kai found himself rewarded with a further two gold sovereigns.

• • •

After lunch, which Big Ben served in the fishing hut and which consisted of young partridges braised in cabbage, Kai went out alone in the boat with Nick Winter.

"You had a tragedy here, I gather?" he said to the ghillie.

"We did, sir."

"What happened?" he asked him.

"Lord Embers was a heavy man," Nick answered. "He lost his footing and found himself in the water."

"He found himself in the water?"

"As I say, Lord Embers was a heavy man."

"And he couldn't swim?"

"The river was in spate, sir."

"And there was no one about to save him?"

"I tried to save him."

"But were unable to?"

"I was with him, but to my great regret, which will be everlasting, I was unable to reach him."

That night, their fishing at a conclusion, Kai handed Nick all of the gold sovereigns that he had won from the King the previous day. As he did so he felt a great sense of sadness, but also one of relief.

"I am much obliged to you," Nick said, pocketing the coins.

• • •

As they dressed for dinner later that evening, Constancia tried to make love to Kai.

"I shall face the forests again, only this time I shall pretend you have taken me unawares. I shall struggle a little, but you will succeed in your endeavours," she laughed her coquettish laugh.

Except Kai was unable to partake.

"What is it, Kai?" Constancia pressed him. "What's the matter? Why are you so subdued?"

"I feel sadness for Nick Winter," Kai replied.

"Why?"

"Because he was responsible for the death of Lord Embers."

"Who is Lord Embers? And what do you mean by implicating Nick Winter, the quiet man I like so much?"

"Lord Embers was the King's private secretary, the man who drowned on the river. And Nick Winter was responsible."

"Don't speak such nonsense! How can you possibly know that?"

"I can tell."

"How?"

"I had a vision. I saw what happened."

"Then what *did* happen?"

"Lord Embers and Nick Winter were alone in the boat. They quarrelled. And Lord Embers lost his life by drowning."

"What a lot of rot!" Constancia laughed.

"But you yourself had a dream in the rainforest about a boat and Nick Winter, did you not? And of a dog and catching it on a line."

"You think that is of significance?"

"Most certainly, I do."

"What a fey man you are! You believe we dream from the same pool?"

"I would find it just as hard to believe we do not."

• • •

Constancia wasn't in the least interested in this story of Kai's. In fact, it only made her want to make love to him even more. One by one over the next four days they stole into the empty bedrooms on their corridor, as it was only in a new room that Kai was able to become aroused.

And each day at the conclusion of fishing, Kai would hand the ghillie all the gold sovereigns he had won from the King the previous evening.

• • •

On the fifth day of their visit the King had a horse running in a local point-to-point. Wishing to go incognito, he planned to arrive disguised as an old man, his face wrapped in a scarf, his head covered with a wide-brimmed fedora. And thinking he would be recognized if he spoke, he sent Kai to place a bet on his behalf with a handful of gold sovereigns.

This was Kai's second challenge. It was difficult now not to think there was an agency at play. Again and again his sobriety was being put to the test.

It was not such a straightforward matter placing the wager, however. The gold sovereigns may have been legal tender, but none of the bookmakers would touch them.

Except for one.

"These are the King's sovereigns, aren't they?" this bookie asked, staring at the mound of gold in his hand.

"Yes," Kai had to answer.

"Then tell me: is the King here today?"

"That I am not at liberty to say."

"Not at liberty to say! That's as may be, but I will only take this bet if, should it convert, the King comes in person to collect his winnings."

This seemed to Kai a good solution, as it would not necessitate him handling the coins again, he thought.

"Fine," he said.

Except the King would not hear of this plan when Kai related what had happened.

"How could I possibly go in person to collect my winnings from one of my subjects, as you suggest?"

"It wasn't my suggestion, Sir," Kai corrected him, "it was his."

"Go back at once and have the rascal return my money."

Kai tried to remonstrate with the bookmaker, who wouldn't hear of returning the stake, referring Kai to a poster on which, in small text, was listed his company's Terms of Business. Kai found himself in a terrible dilemma. If the horse should win and the King was unable to collect his winnings, then that, in effect, was the same as a lost stake.

In the heat of the moment – the horses were under starter's orders and the race was about to begin – he reached into his own pocket and placed a bet with the bookmaker with sufficient of the notes he had in his wallet to cover what he thought the King would be due should his horse cross the line first. It was strange when he thought about it later: not once was he properly aware of what he was getting himself into.

Luckily, the horse did not win. It fell at the third fence from home. Kai had been too agitated to return to where

Constancia and the King were standing by the final hurdle, a position from which they planned to cheer on the royal hunter. He was halfway there when he saw the King's horse unseat its rider, the jockey wearing the royal colours taking a terrible tumble.

"Well, well," the King said ruefully as finally Kai approached them, "a good job we got our sovereigns back, then."

Kai had to tell the King what had happened.

At first the King flew into a rage. "He wouldn't give my sovereigns back?"

"No, Sir."

Then he started laughing, a deep belly laugh.

"So what? Anyway, I never win! That's doubtless why the bookmaker wouldn't return my money. Not only did he know I wouldn't come in person to collect my winnings, he knew that any wager of mine was as good as a banker seen from his side of the fence."

• • •

Back in London Kai went straight to a meeting of *Gamblers Anonymous*.

"I'm struggling, I have to be honest with you," he told the group. "Things aren't the same at all. I came here a week ago, confident, full of myself after my adventures in the jungle . . . as I see it now I was riding for a fall . . ."

There was a murmur of laughter at the use of this metaphor.

"I am totally confused . . . at sea. To cut a long story

short I was staying with a person of some renown in Scotland – this being an anonymous meeting I'm not at liberty to say who this person was, although he will be familiar to you all – and at every juncture, whether it be mini-golf, fishing, or backing an old hunter of his that was racing in a local point-to-point . . . it really didn't matter what . . . this man was determined to wager. And at every juncture, fool that I was, I was party to it. Of course, this personage being one of the richest and most fortunate in the land, this gaming had nothing to do with money. I know that, he knew that. But why now, if I have that level of insight and awareness, should my life be turned so upside down?"

The room had gone very quiet, Kai realized, as the members listened with interest and sympathy. In the front row there was seated the same man who had been so attentive and courteous when Kai had attended the meeting a week before. This man's patient and knowing expression encouraged Kai to go further.

"The worst of it is I have come back with a stain," he went on uncertainly, but knowing somehow he must continue. "There had been a terrible tragedy on my host's estate – a man had drowned in a boating accident on the river there. Only I am convinced it was no accident."

• • •

After the meeting Kai and Cal went for coffee. Cal tried to reassure Kai with the usual platitudes.

"Gambling is a cunning and baffling disease. You've

had a slip: there's no more to it than that. It happens to all of us. So what? You've learnt you weren't cured in the jungle? You've always got this fellowship. And as for this business about the accident on the river, forget about it: it has nothing to do with you."

"I wish it were as simple as that."

"Then what's the problem?"

"The accident on the river is not my business, as you say, but a man's life was lost, and that is something of significance. I regret the instant I stepped foot in the King's castle . . . I am not the same person I was before I crossed that threshold."

At this Cal was understandably shocked. "You mean you were a guest of the King?" he whispered.

"Yes."

"The King of England?"

"This is an anonymous fellowship and it was wrong of me to have identified my host. Please forget my indiscretion."

And here Kai would speak no more of his week in Scotland.

The Hargreaves Twins

Not far from where Kai and Cal had been drinking coffee, a woman lay dying on the top floor of a hospice. Her name was Edith Hargreaves and seated by her side was her twin sister, Gwendoline Hargreaves.

There had been a history of competition between these sisters. This had reached a climax on their eighteenth birthday, when both had applied for a position within the Royal Household. And both being good candidates, it had been difficult to know how to proceed. In fact the King himself had had to step in. He was like that: reluctant to allow others to undertake difficult tasks on his behalf, he always liked to officiate when there was something of a sensitive nature to decide.

On the day in question he had decreed that the toss of the coin should settle the matter.

"I can't think of another way," he said. "If anyone else can I would be pleased to hear from them."

So he tossed a coin, a special sovereign kept for these occasions, and it had landed **HEADS**.

"Edith it is," he pronounced.

Of course this hadn't done much to ease the tension between the Hargreaves sisters, since their rivalry was underpinned by a jealousy and resentment made unyielding by the years. In fact it wasn't until Gwendoline, the "loser" in that game of chance, qualified as a vet that she was thankfully free of that sense of injustice, a sense of injustice which had only been made worse – if truth be told – by the fall of the coin.

• • •

It may all have been a long time ago, but as she sat at her sister's side, Gwendoline had time to revisit that earlier rivalry. The worst of it had been to do with travel, she remembered. The years before she qualified into veterinary practice she would imagine her twin on the royal yacht. She might be crossing the Atlantic Ocean, arriving on the Hudson Bay just in time to see the Statue of Liberty take shape through a sea mist. Or she might picture her sister walking off the royal gangplank somewhere in the South Seas, to be greeted by women in grass skirts.

Little did she know it but Edith had continued to suffer, too. And this in spite of the coin falling in her favour. It had been no secret that of the two Gwendoline had been their parents' favourite; and Edith had wrongly assumed that her appointment to a position within the Royal Household would elevate her above these feelings of loneliness. It hadn't, though. Indeed sometimes she felt more alone than ever as she walked the miles of corridors that stretched, like arteries, through each of the royal residences.

• • •

Presently a nurse came into Edith's room to administer painkillers. This was done via a syringe driver, positioned out of view beneath the blankets. (She may not have known it – or cared, for that matter – but time was running out for Edith: these drugs had been prescribed to afford a peaceful and dignified end to her suffering.)

"Edith, are you awake?" the nurse whispered. "Can you hear me? You have a visitor."

Edith managed to open her eyes. "A visitor?" she mumbled. "Who?"

"His Majesty, The King of England."

In her scramble to haul herself up against the pillows, Edith nearly sent the syringe driver crashing to the floor.

"The King," she gasped, "quick, Gwendoline, the King!"

This must have been all the King was waiting for, because a few moments later he was in the room. He was wearing a long white raincoat and was accompanied by two bodyguards.

"I wished to come and pay my respects, Edith," he began. "I trust and pray you do not object?"

Edith was unable to reply: whether she was recovering from shock or withstanding a wave of euphoria from the analgesics it was unclear. So Gwendoline found herself answering on her sister's behalf.

"Your Majesty, of course she does not object. She may appear to be sleeping, but I'm certain she is aware of your presence."

"You see, she has been such a long-standing and loyal

member of staff," the King went on with a sad frown. "And so unwaveringly discreet, too. You will appreciate that in my job discretion is so vital. But, of course, I remember you," he went on, a smile lifting the frown as he turned his attention properly to Gwendoline. "Many times I have had occasion to recall that morning when we tossed the coin. And not without a certain sense of regret that we should have had to resort to such measures – and yet, needless to say, wonder of your destiny."

"It was the only way, Your Majesty," Gwendoline did her best to reassure the Sovereign.

"Well, yes, I have always tried to do these difficult jobs myself. But tell me," he asked, "how is your life? I trust you are finding it fulfilling?"

"More than fulfilling, Sir. I have always loved animals and I became a vet."

"A vet! Now there's a job! To alleviate the pain of those who suffer without having the capacity of knowing they suffer."

"Oh, Sir, but many animals are very intelligent," Gwendoline objected.

"Of course they are!" the King agreed. "That is why cruelty to these sentient beings is so doubly unacceptable. They may not possess our ability to comprehend the consequences of pain and suffering, but they do have a great capacity to feel it – not only their own, but that of others as well. Only tell me, if you were so interested in animals, why did you apply for the position of housekeeper at Buckingham Palace?"

"I am ashamed to say it was out of a sense of competition, Your Majesty."

The King gave a knowing laugh. "A rivalry between siblings, you mean?" he asked, taking Edith's pale and limp hand.

"We had rather a bad case of it, I'm afraid," Gwendoline smiled back.

• • •

When the King had gone, Edith awoke from her reverie.

"I dreamt of the King," she murmured.

Gwendoline wasn't sure it would be wise to correct matters. "You did? What did he say?"

"He thanked me for being such a loyal servant. But one thing," the dying twin frowned.

"Yes?"

"He asked me if I had had a fulfilling life."

"And how did you respond?"

"I told him it had been fulfilling – up to a point."

• • •

Edith died later that night.

Gwendoline had wondered whether she shouldn't wait for the event, actually be there in person when her sister took her final breath, as it was clear that the end was very near. But when she had thought about it more carefully, she realized that she hadn't wanted to witness Edith's demise, as it would be akin to witnessing her own. So she had bade her sister a silent goodbye, lingering a moment or two longer at the door so she could give her one last look, before going home.

Malcolm Message

The funeral took place a few days later at Gunnersbury Crematorium. The Royal Household had sent a spray of flowers, modest in size so that it would not outdo any other spray. Its message was brief and modest, too. It read:

"In deepest sympathy, The King."

Gwendoline had organized for a small buffet to be made available at *The Ampthill Arms*, a public house a few streets down from the cemetery; and after the service the dozen or so mourners made their way there through a fine drizzle. It was the publican's habit to light a fire on these sad occasions, and one by one the mourners approached Gwendoline as she sat by the fire's fender. Until at last she was left alone.

Alone, that is, save for a man in a dark overcoat. He smiled weakly at Gwendoline, who smiled back.

"I'm sorry for your loss," he said to her.

"You were a friend of my sister's?" she asked him.

"More an admirer."

"Who are you, if you don't mind my asking?"

"My name is Malcolm Message and I used to know your sister through work."

"You mean you work at the palace?" Gwendoline

questioned him with such discretion Malcolm was scarcely able to catch her words.

"Not exactly. My company had a contract at the palace. I'm not at liberty to divulge the nature of the work, but it would invariably involve dealings with Edith."

"I see. You say 'had'?"

"Unfortunately my company went into liquidation earlier this year and for that reason . . . and others . . . I had rather lost touch with Edith."

"I'm sorry to hear that," Gwendoline said with a sigh. And because there was something about Malcolm Message that she had warmed to, she said: "I'm not sure I want to go home quite yet, I don't know about you? But why don't we sit down and talk a while?"

• • •

In fact Malcolm wasn't as discreet as he made out. That or he instinctively trusted Gwendoline in the way he had instinctively trusted her sister. Until earlier that year he had been Managing Director of the plumbing company that his great-grandfather had founded a hundred years ago, he told her.

"We had the contract at Buckingham Palace since before the war – the Second World War, that is. Did you know the palace has seventy-eight bathrooms? And because it's the palace there's a maintenance schedule for each and every one of them?"

"Seventy-eight bathrooms!" Gwendoline repeated. "No, I didn't know that."

"But, alas, we lost the contract."

"Not on account of my sister, I trust?"

"Oh, good heavens no!" Malcolm reassured her.

"Then how?"

Malcolm was a modest man, a person who did not like to denigrate others. On this subject, however, it was difficult not to be more forthright. Basically there had been some insider dealings at the palace, he said, and a certain member of the Royal Household had stood to benefit from a change of contractors. Malcolm didn't tell Gwendoline this in so many words. Instead he described to her how that member of staff had cited negligence on his company's part and had terminated the contract on that basis.

"But who was this member of staff?" Gwendoline asked him.

Malcolm leaned forward to whisper in her ear: "A gentleman by the name of Lord Embers."

Gwendoline knew the name well: Edith had often spoken of him.

"You mean the King's private secretary?"

"The same man."

They talked on and on, the evening turning to night. Malcolm had never spoken so frankly to anyone before, not even to Edith, whom her sister so closely and uncannily resembled, even down to the same creases about the eyes. He had taken the failure of his business very hard.

"I don't think I shall ever recover from it," he said.

"But it wasn't your fault," Gwendoline had no difficulty in saying.

"Of course it was my fault! It was sheer folly to rely on just one client like that. I should have had other irons in the fire."

"It was Lord Embers who undid you, though."

"So many people's destinies I have had a hand in altering. Oh, how I wish I had never been granted that responsibility."

• • •

In truth Malcolm had been very much in love with Edith Hargreaves. And she in love with him.

And there lay the real problem: Lord Embers, who had an unsatisfactory personal life himself, did not like others to enjoy the harmony and pleasures which to date had eluded him. He sought to destroy love affairs if he became aware of them within his sphere, claiming they posed a threat to the palace's code of confidentiality.

"Lord Embers will interfere if he learns of our liaison," Edith had told Malcolm one night as they sat in her quarters on one of the palace's back staircases.

"Interfere?" Malcolm had laughed.

"I will lose my job and you will lose yours."

"My firm has had the plumbing contract at Buckingham Palace for more than fifty years. As you know it was under my grandfather's stewardship that the current system was installed. We know the position of every stopcock and isolation valve. It will take more than Lord Embers being unhappy with our friendship to bring a conclusion to that. And as far as your job goes: no court in the land would see an employee like yourself be given their cards. You are as safe as the palace itself!"

But Lord Embers had succeeded in wresting the contract from Malcolm. It was said one of his nephews had a controlling interest in the nationwide company that took over from *Message & Sons*. Of course Lord Embers hadn't had a hand in Edith's cancer: that went without saying. But to all intents and purposes he had destroyed their idyll, since once the business was in receivership and once Edith's illness had been diagnosed then nothing was the same again.

Malcolm had found redundancy difficult, almost impossible to manage. He was forty-two, too young to retire, yet able to do so if he wished on the pension he had been careful to provide for himself. Only guilt tortured him. At one of the consultation meetings that had taken place during the winding up of the business, his outspoken secretary, a woman by the name of Brinet Mills, had stood up and said: "You've wrecked a lot of people's lives, you know."

Wrecked a lot of people's lives! How he wished he had never been granted the responsibility over others!

• • •

Yet, as he returned to his flat that night after bidding Gwendoline farewell at the *Ampthill Arms*, Malcolm found he had a new spring in his step. Until the early hours he lay in the semi-darkness, strangely conflicted. What was it he found so attractive about Gwendoline, he kept asking himself. Was it the depth of her smile, which in its fullness was even more beautiful than Edith's? he wondered.

At last he fell asleep, only to have the strangest dream.

He dreamt he was early for his annual appointment at the palace to renegotiate the plumbing contract *Message & Sons* had once enjoyed, and after taking two turns around the Victoria Memorial, he had taken a seat on its coral-white steps. Presently a man with a cat carrier came to sit beside him. It was a still July morning, and the man spent some time repositioning the carrier so that it was in the shade.

"Close day," Malcolm said to him.

"Isn't it?" the other returned.

Malcolm liked the look and sound of this stranger, who in spite of the warm weather was wearing a thick overcoat.

"Just been to the vet?" he asked him.

"No, in fact."

"On your way to the vet, then?"

The stranger hesitated before answering. "I shouldn't really be telling you this, but I've come to collect the cat . . . from there," he explained, indicating the building before them. "He was born at the palace and we were given him as a kitten, but he won't stop going back there."

"Cats are like that," Malcolm commiserated with his new acquaintance. "Have you tried smearing butter on its paws?"

"Mrs. Hargreaves did suggest we try that."

At the mention of Edith's name, Malcolm became very quiet.

"I've not offended you?" the stranger asked.

"Mrs. Hargreaves and I were friends," Malcolm replied.

"Were?"

"And she died last month."

"I'm sorry to hear of your loss," the man said, bowing his head respectfully.

"Thank you," Malcolm nodded. "You are in fact the first person I have spoken to with such candour."

"Your relationship wasn't an established fact, then?" the stranger asked.

"You're right. We were in love, but it was a clandestine love."

"How so?"

Malcolm indicated the palace. "There were some there who did not approve of our friendship."

The stranger was nodding with interest. "The King's private secretary, you mean?"

"How did you know that?" Malcolm asked him.

"Because I have experienced something similar myself."

And here Malcolm awoke.

Lady Embers

After Lord Embers was drowned on the Dee, his wife made plans to sell the property they owned in Kensington in order to purchase a house south of the river. Her friends may have pitied her, but in fact she was perfectly happy. She had never really loved Lord Embers, and when he died she did not miss him in the least.

At first she felt shame at her lack of remorse, a sentiment she was reluctant to share. Until one day, walking in Hyde Park with a friend, she opened her heart.

"I wish I felt more, but I can't say I do."

"Grief is like that. Don't be too hasty to say how you feel," the other counselled her.

"Perhaps I didn't love my husband?"

"Of course you did! And you shall fall in love again."

"I think that very unlikely."

"Oh yes, but you will! Besides, you will need a man in the house."

"Oh, but I won't!"

"What about the children?"

"What about them? My husband's life was well insured. And, anyway, we have the King, who is to be godfather to one of the twins."

It was the first time Lady Embers' friend had heard of this arrangement. "He is? To which one?"

"That has yet to be decided."

• • •

Later that month the King paid Lady Embers a visit. It wouldn't have done to be so candid with her royal visitor, so Lady Embers sat with eyes averted.

"It's the children I worry about, of course," she kept repeating.

"I'm glad you've brought up the subject of the children," the King went on, "because it brings me to the other reason why I've driven down here today, beyond offering my condolences to you, of course, dear lady. You will be aware Lord Embers asked if I would be godfather to one of your twins?"

"He had mentioned it, Your Majesty," Lady Embers replied.

"At first, if I'm to be honest, I was a little reluctant. Do you know I have sixteen godchildren, Lady Embers?"

"That's quite a number, Sir."

"Exactly your husband's words!"

(Which wasn't strictly speaking true: it had been Nick Winter who had used this expression.)

"But, of course, I would be honoured to be godfather to one of the twins," the King went on quickly. "The only question is – which one?"

"I've thought about that, too, Sir," Lady Embers

said, looking up properly for the first time. "And I was thinking . . ."

"Pray, Lady Embers, tell me what you were thinking?"

"That perhaps you could be godfather to them both?"

"But that would make eighteen!" the King exclaimed.

"Not that I think it would matter in the least if Hannah alone were your goddaughter," Lady Embers quickly backtracked, thinking that the King might be about to withdraw from his obligation. "Or would you prefer to be godfather to Robert?"

"It so happened that once before, Lady Embers, I had to choose between twins," the King said, taking the special golden sovereign from his pocket, "and we settled it with this."

"You mean on the toss of a coin?" Lady Embers frowned.

"I can't think of a better way. If *you* can, I'd be glad to hear of it."

Lady Embers couldn't think of a better way, so the coin was tossed. It landed **HEADS**, which meant that Robert, and not Hannah, would be the King's newest godchild.

• • •

About a week later Lady Embers was deadheading some roses in her front garden, when she was approached by a tall, casually dressed young man.

"Are you Lady Embers?" this man asked her in a pleasant American accent.

"Whose business is it if I am?" she haughtily replied.

"My name is Kai Nelson. I'm from northern California and I would like to speak with you."

Lady Embers was sufficiently intrigued to invite the stranger into the hallway of her house.

"Pray, tell me the nature of your business," she asked once they were both over the threshold.

"I'm afraid you may find what I am about to say to you upsetting," Kai began.

"I will be the judge of that."

"Indeed for some time I have wrestled with whether I should come and see you or not . . . "

"Well, now you are here, you had better get on with it," was the rejoinder.

"The fact of the matter, Lady Embers, is I don't think your husband's death was an accident."

"You don't?"

"I am convinced there was more to it than is known."

Lady Embers sat down with her back to the dark stranger. This was a way of concealing her feelings (or lack of them); it also gave her time to consider what she had been told. Her first anxiety was with regard to the life insurance payment she was about to receive. If there were an investigation, this might make matters difficult.

"What you have said has shocked me beyond description," Lady Embers whispered once she had regained her composure. "You'd better explain yourself. How do you know this? And who else knows?"

"No one knows of my suspicions apart from a young woman from Argentina, who was also a guest at the castle."

"And what woman would that be and what castle?" Lady Embers demanded to be told.

And so Kai explained the story from beginning to end. How he had met Constancia in Iquitos; how she had invited him to accompany her on a visit to Balmoral; how he had fished on the very stretch of the Dee on which Lord Embers had met his end; and how he had even met the ghillie under whose charge Lord Embers had been entrusted.

"So you're accusing this poor ghillie of murder!" Lady Embers exclaimed.

"I'm only sharing with you what I sense to be the truth."

"Which amounts to no more than a gut feeling!" Lady Embers interjected with venom. "And pray, why should I even believe you *were* at Balmoral."

At this Kai withdrew a gold coin from his pocket. "This is one of the King's sovereigns," he told Lady Embers.

Without betraying her feelings, Lady Embers took the sovereign. It was identical to those her husband used to bring home some evenings from the palace.

"And how did you come by this?" she asked the young man, scrutinizing him more closely still.

"The King likes to wager and I won it on a bet."

"On a bet?" Lady Embers repeated, trying to hand the coin back to him.

"At every juncture the King was determined to wager. I would like you to keep the sovereign, Lady Embers. I am a reformed gambler myself. I no longer wish to own it."

And with that Kai left.

• • •

Lady Embers sat quietly in her sitting room. It would have been much better if this whole episode hadn't happened, she was thinking. But it had! The story the young Californian had imparted, regardless of whether it was true or false, would remain like a stain, she knew, the kind of stain that would never come out in the wash, no matter how concerted the endeavours to remove it.

And what to do with this gold sovereign? It couldn't be thrown away any more than it could be spent. And so Lady Embers buried it in her back garden, which she did first by placing it in a jam jar, folded up in a piece of paper on which was written the day's date and the following short explanation:

"This coin was given me by a Californian
on his return from Balmoral following
the death of my husband."

II

In The Borders

After that painting was removed from its place outside the rod room door at Balmoral, intimacies between Nick and Angela were never the same again. At first Angela would tease him.

"No more hard Winters?" she would breathe in his ear.

To which Nick could make no reply.

Then, feeling rejected, she became less playful. "A woman needs a man," she reminded him.

• • •

Eighteen months later the situation came to a head when, taking the long back way back to Balmoral from the coast one afternoon, Nick spied Angela's car parked off-road, not far from where one of her childhood lovers lived, a forester by the name of Walter Eliot.

"You're seeing that man again?" he asked his wife to confirm later that evening.

"Sometimes," Angela admitted.

"Why?"

"Because I am no longer satisfied," she replied.

• • •

It was a difficult divorce. Their children were too young to understand why their parents were planning separate lives, and it had taken the efforts of a social worker to help create a new status quo. Only this was beset with problems, too. The mediator, named Heather, had taken a fancy to the spurned husband, and sometimes they would meet clandestinely – Heather was married to a policeman – and try to make love in Nick's car.

"You are like the lion in the Wizard of Oz," she would tease him, buttoning back up her blouse over her ample bosom, "you have lost your courage."

"I know," Nick would meekly reply.

"You must act! Otherwise you will find the years have gone."

• • •

Determined to start afresh – and to put some distance between himself and his wife who had moved into her lover's cottage close by – Nick took a job as ghillie in the Scottish Borders, on an estate owned by a rich American who went by the name of Richardson. Mr. Richardson had made his fortune in surgical hardware and, judging by the amount he and his guests were rumoured to tip the servants at the Big House, a large fortune it must have been, too. In fact often the servants, Nick included, would wonder if actually Mr. Richardson wasn't richer than the King of England himself.

• • •

Soon after his relocation, Nick had a dream, a dream he was to have again and again over the ensuing years.

He dreamt he was baling out the boat in preparation for a day's fishing on Mr. Richardson's beat, and when he looked up it was to find a teenager staring down at him.

"And who are you?" he gruffly asked.

"I'm Lord Embers," the boy replied.

"The devil you are!" Nick growled.

"Oh yes, I am! And Mr. Richardson has told me I shall be under your care today. He will be down presently. I will let him tell you himself."

And with this the young man stepped into the fishing hut and busied himself with assembling his rod.

The present Lord Embers was right: Mr. Richardson was down before long, accompanied by Lady Embers.

"Good day to you, Mr. Winter," the laird began in his easy manner. "Tell me if I'm mistaken, but the water looks decidedly promising this morning. You've met young Embers, I see; it only remains for me to introduce you to his mother, Lady Embers."

Lady Embers may not have cared so much for her late husband, but she was exacting about matters relating to her son's safety.

"He's to wear a life jacket at all times," she told Nick, "and never to stand in the boat. Our family is no stranger to accidents, you see."

"Yes, ma'am."

"My son is to do exactly as you say, Mr. Winter – I am placing my confidence entirely in your hands."

"Very good, ma'am."

Once in the boat the young Lord Embers was quick to inform Nick of some facts he already knew – and some he didn't, besides.

"I am the King's godson, did you know?"

"Is that a fact?"

"We are often guests at Balmoral, but the King will not allow me to fish his beats. You see about the time I was born there was a senseless accident and my father was drowned. That is why the King has organized it that I come to fish here instead, me being the keen angler I am."

"I see, sir."

"So come on, my good man, let's catch a fish."

In the dream Nick Winter liked the present Lord Embers: he had nothing of the arrogant nature of his father. Even the way he carried himself in the boat, instinctively tuned to the balance of the swell, was so unlike the ungainly manner, slack-shouldered and heavy-footed, his late father would stumble about in the prow.

Presently they were into a fish, and presently it lay dead on the floor of the boat between them, a gleaming bar of silver.

"That's the prettiest fish I ever caught," the young Lord Embers said to Nick, proffering a gold sovereign, "and I would like you to have this."

"I can't take that, Lord Embers."

"You must. I won it from the King last week. It's yours."

At this point, the dream would always end.

South of Eureka

These had been problematic years for Kai, too, with gambling at the heart of his difficulties. Many "fortunes" he had won and many "fortunes" he had lost. He was now living on the Lost Coast in northern California, in a place so open and empty it was possible to lose yourself in the vast scenery of gold. Or to blend amongst the giant sequoias of the Redwood Forest and, in that way, achieve invisibility there, too.

Needless to say, chance had had a hand in his destiny. Down on his luck and living in penury in Reno, the daughter of a casino manager had first taken pity on Kai, and then fallen in love with him. There was something about his honest gait, his loose shoes and corduroy shirts, which she had found deeply irresistible. Soon they were betrothed.

The bride's name was Natasha, and she and Kai were married in a small church above Yosemite Park. Kai's father-in-law was as generous in his financial settlements as he was shrewd: to prevent money from being lost it was put either in his daughter's name or in trust for the grandchildren he anticipated from the union. And as for somewhere to put down roots? Kai had friends who lived in Humboldt County, an area south of Eureka. A simple and rewarding life could be led there in hills overlooking the Pacific Ocean, they told him: build your own home; raise your own stock; grow in abundance everything you might need for the kitchen.

So this was where they settled.

• • •

One night Kai gave a dinner for everyone who had helped him build this home. The party was assembled outside on the terrace of stone. The river was in spate below them, and when the wind changed you could hear its roaring. The sky was black as pitch; clouds raced across a full moon.

"It's difficult to comprehend that when I came here just a few years ago I had no knowledge of carpentry . . . and now look at this beautiful house you have helped me to create from the lumber – the sequoia, cedar, pine, cherry and walnut – we have sourced from these valleys. I thank you from the bottom of my heart. To work with my hands has brought me freedom from obsession. It has taught me to live simply, to see the simplicity in everything about me, to feel whole."

But once the house was completed Kai found he did not feel so whole. It wasn't that he wished to return to the gaming tables, it was more that familiar sense of being unable to concentrate. Sometimes he would try to read a book on the terrace he had helped to construct – only to find himself standing up almost immediately to attend to any number of trivial jobs that could wait.

• • •

One night he dreamt of Balmoral and of the King. The two were seated in the drawing room there overlooking the river, which unlike the river that wound beneath Kai's house in California was absolutely silent.

"I hear you are married now?" the Sovereign asked him.

"That's right, Sir."

"Perhaps you will ask me to be godfather to one of your issue?" the King then suggested.

"I will need to ask my wife about that," Kai replied.

"I am very proud of all my godchildren. Especially the present Lord Embers."

At this Kai awoke in a sweat. He sat beside the open window to stare out at the valley below. Lord Embers! How long had it been since he had heard that name? Ten years? Twelve years? Possibly he had banished it the afternoon he startled Lady Embers in her garden in Tooting – the time he had presented her with that golden sovereign, as if this was the vehicle for transferring the hex he felt had been visited upon him.

• • •

The following morning, first thing, he went to see a healer high up the valley, in a place so remote it had to generate its own electricity.

"I have no compulsion to gamble," he told the healer, "but I feel so distracted."

The healer looked sympathetically at Kai. "My friend," he said, "if you are distracted in this place then action must be taken."

"What kind of action?"

"You say you have knowledge of a crime?"

"A murder, yes."

"Then it is this that is at the heart of your problem. You will not find peace until you find closure with respect to this knowledge you harbour within your soul."

"But how can I prove the killing? Especially now that so much time has elapsed. And what good will it do to the King's godson, the present Lord Embers, who I imagine must nearly be a teenager by now."

"You must confront the boatman you have told me about. This man called Winter. You must let it be known to him you know of his crime. It was your mistake not to have done so at the time. What can have stopped you?"

"Uncertainty," Kai replied.

"And look where your uncertainty has brought you now!"

In Norfolk

Time had done no favours for Malcolm Message, either. With no job to travel to each morning, he soon fell prey to depression and dark thoughts. And whenever Gwendoline, whom he had married soon after their meeting in the *Ampthill Arms*, reminded him of this, he only flew into a rage.

"What can I do here on the coast in Norfolk? There are only so many days of bird-watching a man can countenance."

"You were a manager of people once, a person with considerable administrative skills," the other would try to encourage him. "You could volunteer some hours to a charitable organisation. Who knows the difference you'd make? And there's the best of it: you needn't even know the good you were doing. You would just be doing for the sake of doing!"

This would incense Malcolm. "For the sake of doing!" he would unreasonably retort.

• • •

And then one day Malcolm fell and broke his hip. The doctor on the ward spoke to him in no uncertain terms.

"A broken bone like this can be a turning point, Mr. Message," he told him. "You will need to dig deep, find something to live for."

But there was nothing to live for beyond his smouldering obsession with the past. Malcolm would sit, wheelchair-bound, in the south-facing conservatory of Gwendoline's cottage with its carapace of smoky flint. Sometimes it would become unbearably hot in there, almost too hot to breathe. In those moments his hatred for Lord Embers knew no bounds. Lord Embers had lost Malcolm his business. He had destroyed the idyll he had enjoyed with Edith, breaking their love like a butterfly on a wheel. It didn't seem to improve matters that His Lordship was dead: quite the opposite, in fact. His death, it seemed to Malcolm, had only cheated him of a means of avenging the wrongs he had done. As if Lord Embers had wrought all the damage he could, before turning his back to walk through an open door.

Gwendoline, for her part, quickly regretted her marriage to her sister's admirer. What a fool she had been to forego her independence! There may have been something she had liked about him the day he had introduced himself to her in the *Ampthill Arms*, his modesty and unassuming manner, but there was nothing she cared for about him now. She would walk on the mud flats, dreading her return to the house – her very own house, no less – where Malcolm would be waiting for her, like a chick in a nest, beak open, draining her of her strength and resources.

• • •

The situation deteriorated further. To the point where it became apparent it wasn't so much that Malcolm couldn't walk again after his hip had mended – it was more he didn't want to walk again. Gwendoline had bought him a vast bed with drop-down sides, which resembled a child's cot. One day, he pulled himself up in this bed in the manner of having something important to announce. Such was his state of self-pity that Gwendoline knew what he was going to say before he said it.

"I want to die."

It was a beautiful morning: low clouds were racing across the sea, sweeping it, like a broom. Gwendoline sat there, as still as a statue. On the one hand how could someone make such a statement? On the other it was clear that Malcolm's dying would release them both.

"Did you hear what I said?' Malcolm whispered.

"I did."

"Then will you assist me?"

"By helping you reach Switzerland?"

"That is all I ask."

It was more easily accomplished than Gwendoline anticipated. Malcolm had other medical conditions besides a screwed hip: put together they formed a compelling picture of someone suffering needless pain. The local GP, who was a religious man, was shocked and would have nothing to do with it; but the gentleman in Switzerland to whom Gwendoline spoke by phone was perfectly reasonable.

"Bring him over next month," he said.

• • •

The morning Malcolm and Gwendoline set off for Zurich was cold and dark. They hardly exchanged a word during the journey, flying through dense cloud most of the way. Perhaps that was what death was like? Malcolm didn't go any further than wondering. When one passed, one would simply be suspended in a weightless, aura-like substance of indeterminate colour.

Gwendoline was tortured by conflicting thoughts. How had this unfolding tragedy come to pass? What had she done to deserve it? But what a sense of release she would feel when it was all over, she couldn't keep herself from thinking. In just a few hours she would be on the return leg of her journey – alone and longing for the silence of her flinty cottage.

A people carrier was awaiting them on the tarmac – it seemed Customs was waived for people like Malcolm – and they were whisked to an industrial estate on the fringes of a cold and uniform town of terracotta brick. Again Malcolm stared blindly through the light drizzle; but as soon as they reached their destination, a low building that resembled a Portakabin, he became agitated. So agitated, in fact, that he would not leave the vehicle.

Gwendoline went ahead to explain the situation. This was quite normal, the two receptionists were quick to reassure her; and together they winkled Malcolm through the sliding door of the people carrier and into a wheelchair.

Once inside the low building, Gwendoline and Malcolm were taken into an area of soft furnishings, adorned with ferns and photographs of landscapes, where tea was offered. It was the business of *which* tea that agitated Malcolm further. Would he like herbal, Earl Grey or even 'builder's tea'? the receptionist asked in a thick accent. Suddenly he took in his surroundings properly. How many other people, like lambs to the slaughter, had been asked which tea they would prefer? How many other people had sat in this exact same spot, waiting to go through that exact same door – wherever it led?

"I don't wish to die," he blurted.

The receptionists assured Malcolm that many of their clients had had similar misgivings. But once they had regained their equilibrium they had been perfectly happy with their initial resolve.

"No, you see, I don't wish to die," Malcolm repeated, and thinking he was in danger, he tried to stand.

"Mr. Message, sit yourself down and just take a minute."

"You see I can walk," Malcolm suddenly realized. "I'm not a cripple. Take me home."

• • •

Once they were back in their Norfolk cottage, Malcolm said to Gwendoline: "I must speak to the King."

So Gwendoline telephoned the palace and spoke to Big Ben.

"We've just today returned from Norfolk ourselves," Big Ben informed her, "and, as you know, the King is not overly fond of the countryside around Sandringham. For that reason he has no plans to return there in the near future, so it would be better if Malcolm Message were able to come to London. I'm sure the King would be only too happy to see him."

"Thank you, we shall make arrangements forthwith," Gwendoline told him.

• • •

Malcolm came to have his audience with the King later that week. Only ten days before, he had been confined to a wheelchair; now he was able to walk most of the way to Buckingham Palace from Liverpool Street Station.

The day was fine; the King was taking coffee on the area of flagging outside the French windows that overlooked the rose garden. He was wearing a lounge suit and a pair of loafers.

"Many years have passed, of course," he told his subject, "and much water has gone under the bridge. Nevertheless you were dealt a grave injustice and the shape of your destiny was decided at the hands of one whom one could only call misguided. Will you accept my sincere apologies?"

"I will," Malcolm was quick to reassure the Sovereign. "But I would like to ask one wish that you may be able to grant?" he went on hurriedly.

"I will do all I can to help in putting matters right."

"I should like a job here at the palace."

"But you live in Norfolk, close to Sandringham, unless I have been misinformed."

"I shall no longer be living with Gwendoline Hargreaves. Our union was a mistake from the outset. It was her sister, Edith Hargreaves, I was in love with."

"I remember Edith well," the King mused. "A more loyal servant one could not wish for."

"So you will give me a job?"

"As what, though?"

"I should like to take charge of *Health and Safety* arrangements here at the palace."

"But isn't that a rather lowly job for someone who was once a company director?"

"Your Highness, I was unsuited to the station in which I was born, ill-equipped to compete in the world of cut and thrust. But assessing risks and putting controls in place to mitigate them . . . this was the one area of work at *Message & Sons* that gave me satisfaction. Possibly it should have been my métier."

"Really?"

"This is the contribution I should like to make."

And so the King duly appointed Malcolm Message as *Health and Safety* officer, with a remit to oversee all areas of activity at the royal residences, from construction works to maintenance. With the job came a flat at the top of the palace, which had its own fireplace and coal scuttle. At dusk Malcolm would sit by this hearth, the coals glowing by his side, and stare out through the windows that overlooked St James's Park. He never drew the curtains, as another of his passions was to watch the progress of airplanes as they passed through the inky sky, the silent flashes of light growing dimmer and dimmer, fading like a heartbeat, only to be replaced at the last possible moment by another – and then another.

On The Pampas

Constancia had had a difficult passage, too. She had married the son of one of her father's business associates and had set up home on his estancia north of the Rio Plata. Her husband was away from home a great deal, citing business interests in Buenos Aires as a legitimate reason for his absence. But often Constancia would smell the unwashed clothing he brought back from these trips. Not that she particularly minded his infidelity. She had plenty to keep herself occupied, raising her two daughters, Lucia and Marta, and promoting the estancia as a boutique hotel.

"Why do I have to have truck with these strangers you bring to my home?" her husband, Emilio, would demand in his cups. "Tell me that, after I have worked myself to the bone amongst fifteen million others?"

"I enjoy speaking to them. That is reason enough," Contancia would silence him.

• • •

Then one day the King telephoned.

"I have twenty-three godchildren now and none of them I love more than you!" he began.

Constancia laughed her throaty laugh.

"But I have one to whom I owe a special duty of care: you see he was deprived of his father when he was no more than a babe in arms. He is holidaying in Chile at present, and I think he would enjoy an opportunity to visit your estancia."

"Tell him he is most welcome to call our home his own, Your Majesty," Constancia did the right thing by saying.

• • •

A week later she collected the present Lord Embers from the airport. The name had meant nothing to her when the young man had telephoned from Santiago, but on their way back from the airfield Constancia began to remember that visit to Balmoral all those years ago. Yes, she had gone to Scotland with that strange man, Kai, whom she had met in Peru. They had made love in all the rooms they could on the castle's upstairs landing. But underpinning those days, like a subterranean stream seeping through dark, wet rock, there had been the business of a drowning – of this young man's father, no less – and how Kai had been convinced that a murder had been overlooked. What a strange time it had been!

The days passed pleasantly. The present Lord Embers, who was called Robert – or Rob for short – was a good rider, and Constancia was able to take him on treks far away from the lodge. She enjoyed his easy, confident manner. She also liked the way he was looking at her, stealing glances and then pretending to steal glances. Each day she took him further and further afield, until one day they were sitting beside a crystal-clear pool, where if you sat still long enough you could see the silvery shapes of fish, like ghosts, holding their own against the current.

The tension, as palpable as if it were a scent, was almost too much to bear. The excitement in the young Lord's quivering body, in his flushed cheeks and dilated nostrils, mushroomed like a steed's, was plain to witness; so, too, the confusion in Constancia's voice, in spite of her best endeavours to conceal it. Finally, like a clumsy puppy, he clasped her in the ice-cold water and the spell was broken. In a way she hadn't been able to for years, Constancia gave herself over to passion, to the young man's rough and inexpert touch, which sent shudders down her spine.

If this was a rite of passage for young Embers, it was also a challenge. That night, on their return to the lodge, they found Emilio sitting on the terrace.

"You must be Lord Embers?" the owner of the estancia introduced himself, understanding the situation at once.

"And you must be Emilio?" the young man boldly answered.

All through dinner, through flickering candlelight, the two lovers exchanged furtive glances. What a dangerous game they were playing, Lord Embers knew. But what an extraordinary gift had passed hands.

• • •

Back in the UK, Lord Embers could think of nothing beyond Constancia's long, auburn hair, her exquisite calves, thick eyebrows and slanting eyes. Of the leather chaps she wore during the day and her long flowing skirts at sundown. He would have done anything to return to Argentina! Anything! Little matter his studies and the destiny that was being fashioned for him by his mother and the King of England. His longing was made worse by the fact that his peers did not believe his boasts of seduction and lovemaking in the pampas.

"In your dreams, Embers," they would chant.

Under the stress, Rob's previously good record at school, both in the classroom and on the playing fields, began to suffer. His housemaster called him in for an interview.

"What's the problem, Embers? Unburden yourself."

"I don't like it here any more, sir."

"So you're leaving us?"

"Yes, sir."

"And where do you intend to finish your education, if I might ask?"

"In Argentina."

"Argentina? And why there in particular?" the housemaster pressed him (knowing full well the answer from the gossip he had heard in the masters' common room).

"Because I wish to run a stud farm."

"A stud farm?"

"And I wish to make a start as soon as possible, sir."

• • •

Each night Rob would write to Constancia; and each morning he would wait for a reply. It seemed incredible that none came. Life was not like that! It couldn't be! Or perhaps it was, he was beginning to wonder. He had lost his father in a senseless boating accident, hadn't he? Perhaps that was just what life *was* like: a series of random disappointments, setbacks and, tragedies.

Seeing how he was pining away, never smiling, never laughing, his friends took a more sympathetic view.

"The first cut's always the deepest," they counselled him.

Or: "Be thankful for your initiation."

• • •

There was a reason why Constancia did not reply to those letters: she was pregnant. Since she and Emilio had not enjoyed conjugal relations for over two years, there seemed little point in pretending the baby was his.

She broke the news to him one night over dinner. They were seated alone on the veranda, with Emilio in his usual position at the head of the table. He hadn't shaved that day. The oil from the barbequed meat he was eating was glistening on his stubble. He wore that bullying smile of his, contemptuous and sickly sweet.

"You're not going to tell me it was that runt you were running with," he laughed, throwing a bone to the largest of the ridgebacks they owned.

"What difference is it to you?"

"Well, if he's the King of England's godchild that makes things a little more palatable, wouldn't you say?"

"Leave the King out of it."

"And what do you propose to do?"

There was no question of a termination. "Lucia and Marta will have a sibling. It's as simple as that."

• • •

It wasn't difficult for the present Lord Embers to return to Argentina: he had a good overdraft facility on his bank account and the nature of one who has little difficulty in following through on plans once their mind is made up.

However, no sooner had he landed in this country – which a few months earlier had seemed so benign and full of promise – than he was struck by how alone he felt. He stayed two nights in the Buenos Aires *Continental Hotel*, before flying on to the local airport from which Constancia had collected him on his previous trip. There he toyed with the idea of phoning and asking her to collect him a second time. But what if Emilio answered the phone, it occurred to him only now to wonder. And what about the question of Constancia's silence? Wouldn't it be better to be standing face to face with her than to hear on her voice the surprise and confusion he now so keenly dreaded?

And so Lord Embers hired a driver to take him to Emilio's ranch. Only the driver wouldn't take him as far as the courtyard of hardstanding: he stopped short at the gates to the estancia and would go no further. Lord Embers knew a little Spanish from school.

"Why won't you take me to the house?" he demanded.

"Because this is a bad place," was the answer. "No luck comes to those who find its dirt on their shoes."

Feeling more alone than ever, Lord Embers had no option but to trudge up the three kilometres drive, bearing his luggage. He found Constancia in the garden with her two daughters. Immediately it was apparent to him that she was with child – although not for one moment did it cross his mind that the baby might be his. Constancia could not bring herself to embrace her young lover. She had raised her hands, as if Lord Embers were an apparition.

"Sweet innocent boy, what are you doing here?"

"I have come to see you," Lord Embers hopelessly answered.

"But why?"

"Because you did not answer my letters."

"You fool!" Constancia chastised him.

"I am not a fool! I am in love with you!"

Just at that moment Emilio stepped out of the house. Understanding the situation at once, his reptile-like eyes slanted into a menacing grin.

"Lord Embers! What a pleasant surprise!"

"Forgive me, Emilio," Lord Embers muttered, utterly at a loss.

"Forgive you? For what, pray?"

"For not giving notice of my arrival."

"Nonsense! I think thanks would be more in order."

"Thanks?"

"For the pleasure of your youthful company. Young blood is what we need here, isn't that right Constancia?

We might not be so old and infirm – not yet, that is – but we thrive on the next generation coming through. It invigorates us, doesn't it, Constancia? Come on, we must eat, we must drink some wine," he said, snapping his fingers.

• • •

After lunch Lord Embers was shown to the same bedroom he had been given when first he had stayed at the ranch. The windows were open and the shutters closed. He sank into the soft mattress and pulled a quilt of the finest vicuña over him. Notwithstanding the two days he had spent resting in Buenos Aires, it had been a long journey and he fell into a deep sleep. In fact when he awoke it was difficult to know what time it was. He went downstairs, hoping to find Constancia. But it was Emilio who was waiting for him.

"Good morning, Lord Embers!" Emilio greeted him. "Another cloudless day. But then it's true: most days are cloudless here."

"It is morning, you say?" Rob queried him.

"You have slept, like a puppy, for fourteen hours," Lord Embers was informed.

"And where is Constancia?"

"Constancia has had to make a journey to see the doctor. Nothing untoward. It is on account of her being in the family way, you understand. Now Lord Embers, do you ride?"

Lord Embers had none of his father's weight and lack of coordination. In fact he was quite a good rider.

"Well, yes," he answered, if a little uncertainly.

"Excellent! Then perhaps you will help us on the ranch? We are a hand short today, and any contribution you could make would be most appreciated. Besides, you might be interested to see how we earn our bread here."

"I would be very happy to do what I can to help, Emilio."

"That being the case, we shall set off at once."

Even though Lord Embers was given a hat, it was unbearably hot beneath the prairie sun, and by lunch he was completely done up. Indeed when a gaucho stepped forward with a watermelon and topped it with one blow of a machete, Lord Embers found he had hardly the strength to take the slice that was proffered him, let alone lift it to his lips. What a fool he had been to make this journey, he thought. What he would have given to be back in the UK now! Even if that meant forsaking Constancia, forgetting her forever.

After lunch they began to process the cattle they had rounded up into a vast corral. Their job was to separate the calves from their mothers, and soon the air was full of the sound of discord and longing. It wasn't the sun that was so unbearable now – in any case it had sunk behind some distant mountains – but this haunting sound of desperate pining that was almost too much to countenance.

That night Constancia still had not returned from seeing the doctor.

"She has decided she must go shopping," Emilio told

his sunburnt guest. "But we must allow our womenfolk to satisfy their whims, mustn't we, Lord Embers?"

• • •

The following day was a repeat of the previous. Only this time as they set off Lord Embers saw the gauchos had rifles in their saddlebags.

"Do you shoot, Lord Embers?" Emilio asked him.

Lord Embers was quite a good shot, both with shotgun and rifle. In fact with the latter he had won prizes at Bisley.

"I do enjoy shooting, Emilio," he answered.

"Good! Then once our work is done we shall have ourselves a hunt."

They returned to the corral with its unholy chorus of lowing. The job that day was to drive the cows back onto the prairie. This was much harder work than Emilio had made out, since at every opportunity the cows would try to outflank the team of riders – there were more gauchos that day, all of whom fixed the young lord with glassy stares – in their determination to return to their stolen calves. By the time their task was complete Lord Embers was so sore he could hardly stand.

And then there was the shoot. As they were carrying rifles, Lord Embers had wondered what their quarry might be. It turned out to be driven hare. The last of the cows having been pushed out onto the prairie, Emilio and Lord Embers took up position either side of a dried-up water-course, while the gauchos flanked in a vast area and drove the animals, racing through the pampas grass, towards them. The rifle shots rang out silver through the air. Sometimes it took as many as four or five attempts to stop each animal. Of the six hares they had managed to bag, four of them had fallen to Lord Embers' gun.

"You are a fine shot, Lord Embers," Emilio told him.

"Thank you, Emilio. But Emilio . . .?"

"Yes?"

"I really think I should be returning to the UK."

"Why so soon?"

"Because I must go back to college."

"I never had any use for college myself . . . and see how busy I am, both here and in my offices in Buenos Aires. In any case you cannot leave until Constancia returns."

"And when will that be, do you think?"

"I have never been a great one for speculating when it comes to women, Lord Embers. We must wait and see."

• • •

Two more days and two more nights passed and still there was no sign of Constancia.

Before dawn on the morning of the third day, Lord Embers crept onto the landing outside his room, his idea to let himself silently out of the house, walk the three kilometres to the road and flag down the first car he saw. But before he had reached the top of the stairs the two ridgebacks began to growl from their place by the fire's hearth. And then Emilio appeared, so quickly it was as if he had been waiting for him.

"Lord Embers!"

"Emilio, I really must get back to the UK," the young man stammered, his eyes welling up with tears.

"You've not enjoyed our hospitality?"

"I've enjoyed it more than I can say."

"And you can't wait for Constancia?"

It was a mistake to have come, Lord Embers nearly said. "I can't, I'm afraid, Emilio. I really must get back. Everyone will be wondering where I am."

"Of course you must leave."

"Thank you."

"But not before tomorrow."

"Tomorrow?"

"Yes, tomorrow."

"But why tomorrow?"

"Because I have one last thing to show you."

• • •

This time they set off alone. And this time, because Emilio was wearing a pair of reflective sunglasses, it was impossible to see his eyes. After a two-hour ride they stopped to water their horses in a crystal-clear stream. To his horror Lord Embers realized this was the same pool to which Constancia had brought him some months before. In front of him was the same beach of stone on which he had lost his virginity. Emilio sat down. He had removed his spectacles. To his great consternation Lord Embers saw that Emilio's eyes were wet.

"Emilio, whatever is the matter?" he stammered.

"My wife and my children . . ."

"What about them?"

"I have lost them."

"How?"

"You saw yourself how Constancia is in the family way?"

"Yes?"

"The baby is not mine. Another has a hold on her affections."

In that instant the young Lord Embers, until then blissfully ignorant of the part he had played thus far in these proceedings, realized everything about Constancia's condition. He also realized the extreme precariousness of his position.

"Do you really think so?" he asked Emilio, who by now had replaced his reflective sunglasses.

"You know this place is cursed?" Emilio said by way of an answer.

"Cursed? How so?"

"My father purchased the estancia at auction in Mendoza. No one would touch the place when it was advertised in Buenos Aires. It was said that a cuckolded husband had murdered his rival here."

Lord Embers could only see his own terror in the reflection of Emilio's sunglasses.

"It is said he took him out to a remote spot, perhaps as remote as this," Emilio shrugged, waving a hand over the beach of stone before them, "only one would hope perhaps not quite so beautiful. And there he murdered him with a dagger. It is said there were gauchos on hand to bury the body, gauchos so loyal to their master that they could be trusted to hold their peace in this act of ultimate . . . how does one call it . . . satisfaction."

Lord Embers was surprisingly calm. Indeed he took a moment, without moving a muscle, to establish who would have the upper hand if it came to snatching a weapon. Each of their mounts had a rifle in the saddle-bags; and there was the machete lying between them which Emilio had used to clear their way to where they sat overlooking the pool.

"That is why they say the dirt of this place is cursed," Emilio went on, "and why those to whose feet it sticks must suffer misfortune and hardship in measures unknown to those lucky enough not to cross its boundaries."

"But what about the gauchos?" Lord Embers pointed out.

"What about them?"

"They would not come here if they believed in such stories."

"Some of them don't believe," Emilio shrugged, "and some of them don't care. Why? Because they have nothing to lose. But we have something to lose, don't we Lord Embers?"

"It depends what you mean?" the young lord answered back.

"I think you know what I mean. I may have lost Constancia, but you stand to lose much more," was the answer.

When Lord Embers was unable to offer a comment, Emilio went on:

"I shall bring up this bastard child that Constancia is carrying as if it were my own," he said with his menacing smile. "If it is a son perhaps we shall enjoy riding over the pampas together, as you and I have ridden today. If it is a daughter doubtless I shall have less to do with it. But you, Lord Embers, will have to watch from afar. You will never know this child. You will never smell its breath or look into its eyes, wondering what it is it sees. You will know nothing of these pleasures."

"Emilio!"

"Aha, you say to yourself, you did not wish to see this child take its first steps, utter its first words of unconditional love. You think you will return to your Europe and think no more of this place. But let me tell you, chances are this child will come looking for you. It will seek you out and there will be no place for you to hide. Yes, this child will come looking for you, and once it has touched you, like this," Emilio said, tapping the back of his own head, "well, then, perhaps then you will be aware of the curse of this place. Who knows?"

III

James Stanton-Lacy

From the moment Constancia returned to the estancia – a full week after Lord Embers' departure for the UK – Emilio made life impossible for her. So six months after her baby was born, whom she named Mauricio, she left her husband and returned to live with her parents in Mendoza.

Business had not gone well for her parents. Once a team of servants had waited on their every need: now they were only able to employ a single faithful retainer, an old nanny who went by the name of Bárbara.

"You must write to the King of England," Bárbara told Constancia one day. "He will help you."

"I am too proud to accept help. I have made my life what it is."

"Don't be so foolish! The King has more money than he knows what to do with. Ask him for assistance. That is what godfathers are for."

• • •

Constancia did not write to her godfather. In fact several years passed and she did not think of him once. Until one day he wrote to her.

"I shall be visiting Buenos Aires on official business, and it would be delightful to see you, sweet goddaughter."

And so they met at *Hotel Crillon* in downtown Buenos Aires. The King was in one of his disguises. He wore a khaki suit and thick-rimmed dark glasses. At once he saw Constancia's straitened circumstances.

"Tell me everything," he said.

So Constancia put her cards on the table. It had been a mistake to marry Emilio, she told him: she had known that from the day of their wedding. Her husband loved their two older children and was possessive of them; but her third born, Mauricio, he could not tolerate. As soon as the baby was born, Emilio had been determined to make their life a misery.

"Why?" the King demanded in disgust.

"For all my husband's faults – and he has many – I cannot blame him. You see, the child is not his."

"The child is not his? Are you with the father now?"

"Oh, no!"

"May I ask who the father is?"

And so Constancia told the King Mauricio's father was the young Lord Embers.

"Good heavens!" the King exclaimed.

• • •

The King had every reason to sound surprised, as just that spring he had taken on the young Lord Embers at the palace. It had all begun with a hand-delivered letter, which the King had opened in his dressing gown in front of the window overlooking the Victoria Memorial.

"Dear godfather," it read, "I go up to Oxford this autumn, but is there a chance I could find employment at the palace until then? I would like to work where my father worked, to see how his life must have been for him. Yours ever, Embers."

The King took some time to make up his mind. The previous Lord Embers had made such trouble at the palace. What about those on his staff who would remember those slights as clearly as if they had happened yesterday? In the end he did offer Lord Embers a job, but only on condition that he went by another name, James Stanton-Lacy.

In fact the present Lord Embers – whom the King now addressed as James even when they were alone – was quite unlike his father. The epitome of consideration and good manners, nothing was too much trouble for him. The King had thought at first that he should be kept below stairs, and James was given the job of assistant clerk to the kitchens. His task there was to check incoming goods from purveyors, prepare accounts and balance the books for petty cash expenditure. In this last regard he particularly excelled. For the first time in the palace's history every penny was accounted for. In fact only two months after taking the job, James's immediate superior, normally a taciturn Scot, found occasion to praise his subordinate to the King.

"The lad is a positive asset, Your Highness."

And so the King promoted him to a job on the ground

floor. Here he was on hand to ensure the general smooth running of the palace's day-to-day business, especially when it came to running errands. In this capacity he was quite often sent out to the royal jewellers in St James's to collect pieces that the King intended to present as gifts to foreign visitors and such like.

• • •

One afternoon, about six months following the Sovereign's return from his tour of Latin America, James was sent to Leonard's in Piccadilly.

"There is a good piece to collect there," Big Ben told him. "It will be waiting for you. You are to ask for Thomas Hetherrington and you must go with a bodyguard on this occasion. There have been reports of thieves in the area."

So James set out with the bodyguard to Leonard's, and soon found himself in an octagonal-shaped room with Hetherrington, where Hetherrington told him they would have more privacy.

"We have just this morning finished this piece," he said, opening a Leonard's box. "I believe it is for one of the King's godchildren."

"It's beautiful!" James gasped.

Indeed it was. In front of them, on an octagonal-shaped table, was revealed a bracelet of diamonds and rubies with the name *CONSTANCIA* picked out in emeralds. In an instant James was transported back to that heady time on the pampas, and a deep longing to see Constancia was suddenly revealed to him, as clearly as if he had been staring down into a canyon and now its bottom was miraculously in focus. How dull and pointless his life had been since those days of love and passion, he came to know in a flash.

"You are to take care on the streets," Hetherrington advised James, "there have been incidents lately with robbers."

"I shall be well protected by my bodyguard," James reassured the other.

But no sooner had they turned into Green Park for the short walk back to the palace than they were accosted by four men. The bodyguard was well trained in the practice of martial arts and was able to contain the violence of three of the thieves, but the fourth James had to deal with himself.

"Just give me that packet, or I will take your life," the robber growled.

"I will not! And as far as my life is concerned: Try and take it if you can! I am not afraid of you!"

A desperate struggle ensued. One moment the thief had his hands on the buff-coloured packet, the next the two men were apart, fists up. The rage James felt was unlike any he had experienced before. It seemed he was fighting not for a bracelet, but for Constancia herself. Not only did he fend off this thief, he was able to come to the assistance of the bodyguard, who was close to being overwhelmed. In short they returned to the palace heroes.

• • •

"You are everything a Sovereign could wish for. You are loyal, courteous and courageous," the King told James back at the palace, forgetting for a moment he was his godson. "I'm going to present you with a medal for bravery."

"When I was in the jeweller's, Sir, I couldn't help seeing for whom the bracelet is intended," James ventured.

"It is for my goddaughter," the King confirmed. "The same Constancia with whom you stayed some years ago, if my memory serves me correctly. But owing to our arrangement *vis à vis* your going incognito within the walls of the palace and its immediate confines, I would be grateful if you did not greet her. It is my firm opinion that you must not be known as Lord Embers' son. There will be trouble otherwise."

"Will Constancia be coming with her family?" James asked the King in a querulous voice.

"Constancia has had her own troubles," the King explained to his loyal subject. "She no longer has a family."

"No longer has a family? But she had several children . . . "

"When her husband divorced her he was granted custody of the children. I'm afraid times have been hard for Constancia, James. This is why she is coming to stay with me for a while, and that is why I am choosing to mark the occasion with a bracelet from Leonard's."

• • •

Constancia arrived the following afternoon. Dressed in black, she looked like a widow as she stepped from the royal limousine that had been sent to Heathrow Airport to collect her. James was on duty on the ground floor. He watched as she was ushered into the Green Room, where the King was waiting behind the piano. Her flesh was paler than he remembered it. And although there was the same light in her eyes, she didn't look about her with any interest, choosing instead to stare down at the floor when the King was addressing her.

Some days passed in which Constancia barely left her bedroom, only coming downstairs for meals. At every opportunity James would place himself in a position in which he might be recognized. But Constancia paid him no attention. Once she even looked straight through him. Perhaps this was just as well? James thought. Only he can't have really felt that because on the afternoon of her departure he made a bold move. Constancia had come out of the powder room. James was waiting for her in the Great Hall.

"Constancia," he whispered.

"And who are you?"

"James . . . Embers . . . Rob . . ." the young man stuttered.

"It can't be true!"

"But it is."

"I do not want to see you. Or speak to you."

"But you must!"

"Why?"

"Because I need to know about my . . . about my . . ."

Unable to get the words out, James began to weep.

Constancia took pity on him. "Do not cry, Rob," she tried to soothe him. "All is well with your boy."

"I have a son, then?" James gasped.

Constancia was in tears, too, now. "A beautiful boy called Mauricio," she answered him.

"And Mauricio is being raised by Emilio? With Marta and Lucia?"

"I regret to say not."

"Explain, then."

"There was a bitter custody battle. Once the judges, who were in the pocket of Emilio's family, granted him custody, Emilio had Mauricio put up for adoption."

"And you let him?"

"I spent every last peso I had in the fight. But, as I say, his pockets were deeper than mine. Now I must go and you must forget everything I have told you. No good will come of harbouring regret. We must be satisfied with what we have in the present – not what we feel we could have had."

The Gold Sovereign

It was easier said than done, but over time Rob came to understand there was truth in Constancia's logic. In any case what could be done in a practical sense? Nothing. And what good would it accomplish to any of the parties? None.

The weeks passed in relative harmony. It seemed that everyone loved their job at the palace. This hadn't always been the case, of course, and it wasn't long before the older members of staff saw fit to challenge that impression, as if to remind them all that life was not always so straightforward.

On one such day about a dozen members of staff were congregated in the staff common room for morning coffee.

"We had a private secretary here once who made life a misery for everyone," the cook was saying. "This being Buckingham Palace you would have thought a job here would be a job for life. But no! We were lucky to have a chambermaid that stayed beyond a fortnight."

Malcolm Message had only just come into the common room, but he knew exactly about whom the cook was referring.

"You mean Lord Embers, don't you?" he said.

"I do."

"You may or may not be aware, but Lord Embers was the undoing of me, too."

And he began to unburden himself of his former woes. Some of the older members of staff would doubtless remember him from his annual visits to the palace, when he came to negotiate the plumbing contract? he asked them.

Some heads nodded.

"Well, let me give you the whole picture. It was my great-grandfather who founded the plumbing company *Message & Sons* in 1865. We installed each one of the bathrooms and faucets here in the palace. And being the original contractors the company was given the contract of maintenance, which we held for over eighty years. But then Lord Embers came and we found ourselves pushed aside. For what, you ask? I'll tell you for what. Lord Embers was determined the contract be awarded to a company in which he had an interest. There was insider dealing: put simply it was fraud."

Other members of staff who had also suffered at the hands of Lord Embers nodded in sympathy.

"I had to make twelve people redundant. Twelve people's lives put in jeopardy! I don't claim to be a high-flying executive, far from it. But look at all the other independent traders that exist in perfect harmony in this capital of ours. Do you think they're all Board Room directors? Of course not! Only prey to someone like Lord Embers, a boorish bully, these honest people would have no chance. He was a thoroughly unscrupulous and unpleasant man."

James, who was seated in his usual place next to the Belfast sink, could only bow his head. He knew from an aunt how his mother had suffered in the family home, how she had come to stiffen at the mere sound of his latchkey in the front door.

"But he got his comeuppance," the cook sighed.

"The accident, you mean?" another put in.

"What accident?" Malcolm Message asked.

And so the cook appraised the assembled company of the "facts". Lord Embers had been fishing with the King on the River Dee. There had been nothing extraordinary about the condition of the water, yet Lord Embers had drowned before lunch.

"It was said . . ." the cook stopped.

"What was said?" Malcolm Message asked her.

"It was said the ghillie did not save him."

"How so?"

"Lord Embers lost his footing, it was recorded at the inquest. But what was never explained was why the ghillie made no effort to rescue him."

"Were there no eyewitnesses?" Malcolm Message asked.

"None."

"So nobody knows."

"Not for sure, they don't. But they have a pretty clear idea."

• • •

On hearing this, James sought an interview with the King at the earliest opportunity. The royal party was just about to drive to Greenwich to open a municipal building.

"I didn't realize my father was so universally despised," the young man began by saying.

"I found your father a loyal servant," the King was quick to reassure the other. "The counsel he gave me was always sound. I have come to wonder in hindsight whether he wasn't a troubled man. Do you ever speak to your mother about him?"

"Never."

"As I say, with me he was a paragon of patience and understanding. One can only believe that something was tormenting him."

"And is it true that he died on account of carelessness of a ghillie?"

"We will never know, James."

"Tell me what happened."

And so the King related the story he had related to himself any number of times over the years, a story which had become a little distorted in the remembering. It had been a wild October day, he began, and the river was in spate. Lord Embers had got into a big fish and had seen fit to follow it downstream, which meant crossing the river at its most turbulent point. The boat had spun like a saucer, the King demonstrated with the swivel of a palm, and before anyone knew it Lord Embers was in the water.

"You mean the ghillie didn't jump in to save him?'

"My dear James, the Dee is a big river and especially

furious when flooded. From what I was led to believe, your father was already some way downstream by the time the ghillie righted the boat."

"And then?"

"Well, the ghillie beached the boat and raced downstream to save your father, which is in fact the correct procedure. As you know yourself, great care must be taken when trying to rescue a drowning man."

"But he didn't rescue him?"

"Tragically not. From what I understand he had gone too far downstream, and was unable to locate Lord Embers. It was subsequently discovered that his lordship had been 'hanked', as they say in Scotland, by a branch. It was this that drowned him."

James was in tears. He had a father who had drowned in a river and a son who was somewhere – God only knew where – in South America.

"That very morning," the King went on, taking James's hand, "Lord Embers asked if I would have the honour of being your godfather. I like to think that I have been able to make amends for what happened by taking a special interest in your destiny."

"Why amends?" James asked him.

"Foolishly Lord Embers and I had taken a bet on who would catch the biggest salmon that morning. Possibly your father would still be alive today if we had been like ordinary people and gone about our fishing without the frivolity of gambling."

"And where is this ghillie now? Does he still work at Balmoral?"

"Now, James!"

"I would like to meet this man. Not to confront him. No, I would not do that; nevertheless I would like to meet him."

"No good will come of it," the King warned the other.

"Dear godfather, I believe I *must* meet the man to whom my father spoke his last words. I do not mean to make trouble, but until I have actually seen him with my own eyes I don't think I shall ever make sense of what you have just told me. It will stop me getting on with my life."

And so the King told James that the ghillie was called Nick Winter and that he worked now in the Scottish Borders, on a stretch of the River Tweed below St Boswells.

• • •

Before Lord Embers set off for St Boswells he called on his mother, who was now living in Eaton Square in a vast double-fronted house of white stucco.

"What do you know about the death of my father?" he asked her.

"I was not there. How should I know?" she answered him bluntly.

"But you did not tell me about the ghillie. You have allowed me to find this out for myself."

"Your father was a clumsy man. He stood in the boat when he shouldn't have done and found himself in the water."

"Tell me what you know."

"There is no more to know. I can promise you that. The whole business is inconclusive; it was one man's word against the conjecture of another's."

"So I will go through my life not knowing, too."

Seeing her son in such distress, Lady Embers took pity on him. "Well, there is just one thing that might interest you."

"And that is?"

So Lady Embers recounted the story of the Californian, who had accosted her when she had been deadheading roses in her front garden. And how he had come to her with a wild story about what had happened on the Dee. He claimed to have just returned from Balmoral, having been a guest there, even handing her a coin to prove he was speaking the truth.

"And where is this coin now?" the young Lord Embers demanded.

"I buried it."

"You buried it? Where?"

And so Lady Embers finished her story. In the Tooting house she had bought after her husband's death she had ordered the contractors to make an ornamental pond. A path of stone flags led to this pond, and she had buried the coin in a jam jar under the third flag from its edge.

"I didn't know what to do with it. I didn't want to keep it, nor did I want to spend it. And the Californian, who told me he was a reformed gambler, didn't wish to keep it, either."

"So this coin is still there now?"

"How should I know? I have no idea if the present

owners kept the pond," Lady Embers answered, "but if they did . . . Well then, yes, presumably it will still be there."

• • •

This coin became quite an object of fascination for the young Lord Embers. It was all very well this hearsay about his father's demise, especially when overheard in a staff common room. But for there to exist a gold sovereign which a guest had actually brought back from Balmoral at the time of his father's death – this was something tangible.

That night he set off for Tooting to find it. Having been raised in the house he knew exactly how to access the communal gardens from the street, and once inside these gardens he had no problem in scaling the back fence of his childhood home. Lord Embers hadn't brought a spade with him and it was harder to lever the third flagstone from the end than he thought; but, finally, he was able to throw it aside. To reveal, just as his mother had described it, a jam jar containing both the gold sovereign and a note in her handwriting that read: "*This coin was given me by a Californian on his return from Balmoral following the death of my husband.*"

For a moment he was overcome by emotion. All his life he had wondered what it would be like to grow up with a father – his mother had remarried, but this man had never offered the warmth and protection of a blood father – and here in the shape of the sovereign was the essence of that elusive figure. He slumped against a tree and fell into a profound and deep sleep.

He dreamt he was climbing some rocks on a rocky coast. The further he went the more precipitous the climb became, until he reached a point where he could go no further and from which he could not return. He seemed to be accompanied by a dog. It wasn't clear: sometimes the dog would be in front of him, urging him on; at other times it would be some way behind, entreating him to come back with whimpers of warning. Just as he had reached that point where he realized he was in effect doomed, he was awakened by the sound of a real dog barking and someone shining a torch in his eyes.

"And who are you?" a voice demanded. "And what are you doing on my property?"

"My name is Lord Embers and I used to live here."

"The devil you are!"

"My mother buried something in the garden, and I have come to retrieve it."

"Show me what you have retrieved."

"I will not," the young Embers replied, holding the jam jar close to his chest.

"I will make you, then."

And a great fight ensued. Lord Embers was a strong man, as has already been seen. Moreover the coin he was clutching in his hand seemed to invest him with an added power. But the owner of the house was an able man, too, and was quickly threatening to get the upper hand. On account of the noise they were making and the barking of the dog, the hitherto darkened windows of adjoining houses were soon ablaze with colour.

"Stop thief!" one voice shouted over the communal gardens.

"Apprehend that man!" clamoured another.

They were by now rolling on the lawn, the struggle having reached a critical stage. Summoning all of his remaining energy, Lord Embers threw one last carefully aimed blow and was finally able to escape the other's bear-like clutches. The jam jar in his right hand, he dashed through the communal gardens and exited them by the same route he had found entry. But waiting for him was a policeman, and before long Lord Embers found himself in a police station answering to charges of breaking and entering and causing affray.

The police had placed the gold sovereign on the interview room's table.

"My mother buried this coin when she was living in the house," Lord Embers kept insisting.

"And why are you only now seeking to retrieve it?" the police reasonably asked.

"Because I only recently became aware of its existence."

"But don't you realize this is no longer your house; that the coin by default belongs to the new owner."

Lord Embers was disinclined to agree. "The coin belongs to me, it is of great significance. My mother should never have buried it. It was for me to own."

The police were naturally interested to know more about the coin, but here Lord Embers refused to explain further. He knew any mention of the King would be met with ridicule. And in any event this was a private, family matter.

"If you do not explain yourself, then you must spend the night in custody," the police told him. "You will appear before the magistrates tomorrow morning on charges of breaking and entering and assault."

Parker-Jarvis

And so Lord Embers was thrown into a cell in which there was already a prisoner, also awaiting the morning courts. This ruffian was about the same age as Lord Embers, and although he was clearly a rough fellow the two fell into conversation. Lord Embers may have been reluctant to inform the police of his woes, but with this urchin he was more forthcoming.

"Do not worry," this fellow said once Lord Embers had unburdened himself, "you are a good and honest man. Deprived of your father, your only wish is to make sense of your past. Of course I believe your godfather is the King of England! And I can tell you now how appreciative His Highness will be not to have been drawn into your mishaps of last night. But why don't I assist? If the judges do not release you tomorrow, then perhaps I could travel to Buckingham Palace to bring news of your misfortunes."

At the thought of this rogue applying to the palace on his behalf, Lord Embers hung his head in shame.

"They *will* release me tomorrow, won't they?" he cried.

"It depends upon the state of your victim."

"My victim!"

"If he is discharged from hospital and all is well with

him, then the judges may release you. If not, then your crime will be seen as more serious and you can expect to wait here for some time."

• • •

This ruffian, whose name was Parker-Jarvis, had, of course, been all the while plotting to further his own interests. When the following morning he was released and Lord Embers was not, he went directly to the palace.

He was not admitted straight away into an audience with the King: first he laid before Big Ben the story he had spun. Namely that Lord Embers had repaired to a tavern on the south side of the river, where he had become intoxicated and fallen into a drunken row with a team of road sweepers. Lord Embers was a strong man, stronger than perhaps he himself knew, Parker-Jarvis told Big Ben, and he had wrought extensive damage to the pub and had offended any number of people, some of whom were "bad" men and well-known in the neighbourhood as such. As a result he was being "held", and would only be released for the price of a ransom.

"How much?" Big Ben asked Parker-Jarvis.

"Twenty thousand pounds," the other answered.

"That's ridiculous!"

"That's as maybe, but possibly the price is not so great when taken into consideration the shame and embarrassment that will be brought upon the King, should the events of the previous evening be made public. Given the special relationship the King has with Lord Embers, you understand."

• • •

At first, when Big Ben related this story, the King was disbelieving.

"Why should we go along with any of this?" he cried.

"My thoughts exactly, Your Highness. But then there was mention of a gold sovereign."

And Big Ben described the sovereign, which had been the focus of the fight apparently, and how it had been won in a wager (which is as far as Lord Embers had gone in describing it to Parker-Jarvis).

At the mention of the sovereign the King grew very solemn. At first he blamed himself, thinking the information he had furnished regarding the death of the previous Lord Embers had perhaps tipped the younger man into a state of hysteria and upset.

"How foolish I was ever to gamble," he kept saying.

And then he grew pensive. "It would be fatal to pay a ransom," he told his valet. "It would set a dangerous precedent: who knows what might follow? And yet we can't simply stand by and watch. What do you think we should do, Big Ben?"

"I think we must think carefully before we act."

• • •

In the morning the King summoned Big Ben to his bedchamber. He had slept badly for much of the night. It was of little consequence that a pair of swans had appeared on the lake the previous evening, something that normally would be seen as a good omen. In fact today it only added to the King's state of confusion.

"I simply don't know what to do," he said, pulling at his chin. "On the one hand we cannot be seen to be paying ransoms; on the other I don't think I shall be able to sleep soundly again until young Embers is safely returned to freedom."

"Perhaps we should wait," Big Ben tried to counsel his sovereign.

"I don't think so, we must act."

And so saying he went straight to the bureau and withdrew the ermine purse in which was kept the gold sovereigns used to decide matters of this nature.

"But Your Highness, you have been using the coins less and less of late," Big Ben reminded him.

"I am keenly aware of that fact," the King replied, "but with matters relating to the young Lord Embers I think we must take a longer view. The fact is a wager in all likelihood cost the previous Lord Embers his life. In trying to win a bet he took undue risks. By submitting to chance this decision in how to act on behalf of his son, don't you see we are putting matters to right?"

"But what if the coin gives the wrong answer?"

"Who are we to say what is the right or wrong answer?"

And with these words the King tossed the coin, which

landed **HEADS** and which meant that the ransom should be paid.

Big Ben still had grave misgivings, however. "You are absolutely sure you wish to be guided by chance in this way in a matter of such importance?" he asked one last time.

"I know I have been depending on the coins less of late, yet never more certain have I been than now that we should carry out its instructions."

• • •

And so Big Ben was given an envelope containing twenty thousand pounds. At first he argued that his movements should be monitored by the palace's security: in this way the identity of the kidnappers could be established. But the King would not hear of it.

"If you do not go, I will go myself in disguise," he said.

So Big Ben went to the tavern south of the river. It was sunken beneath the road and so dark it was almost impossible to see with whom he was speaking.

"I have come to see Parker-Jarvis," he said to the publican.

"Who shall I say is asking for him?"

"Just mention the word Embers."

Big Ben had to wait some time for Parker-Jarvis to be found. The publican brought a jug of ale and some beef sandwiches in white bread, neither of which Big Ben touched for fear of being poisoned. Finally Parker-Jarvis appeared. He was surprised and suspicious, but being a canny fellow did not betray his feelings.

"So where is Embers?" Big Ben asked him.

"That is for me to know," Parker-Jarvis curtly answered. "Where is the money?"

"How will I know if I give you the money you will release Lord Embers?"

"You won't. You will have to trust me."

"Why should I trust you?"

"Because Lord Embers is in trouble with some unsavoury characters. I will go as far as to say that if you don't pay the ransom, things will not look so good for the young Lord. The Thames is a treacherous river: many a soul has been lost in its depths . . . unable to support their weight, you understand."

And here Parker-Jarvis wrapped a sinewy hand around his ankle in a menacing manner. His expression was so devoid of feeling that Big Ben handed over the money, which he had concealed in a copy of *The Evening Standard*.

"I shall let the relevant parties know," Parker-Jarvis said, taking the rolled-up newspaper. "Lord Embers will be released forthwith. He may well be back at the palace before you yourself return."

• • •

Lord Embers was indeed back at the palace by the time Big Ben returned. But not released on receipt of the ransom, it was quickly established, rather on bail by the police.

"We've been duped," the King told Big Ben in the Green Room, where both he and Lord Embers were standing beside the grand piano. "We have paid these felons a handsome ransom. Who knows what they will do next."

Lord Embers was very contrite. "This is entirely of my making, and the blame must stop with me. I don't know why I confided in a criminal in the way I did. The last thing I wished to do was to bring disrepute upon the palace; but look what I have done!"

"I am as much to blame," the King sighed with genuine remorse. "If I have set a precedent by paying this ransom then I alone am responsible for whatever may follow."

"But this would never have happened if it weren't for my actions! If ever there was a lesson to be learnt from this sorry story of misadventure it is for me not to pursue any details relating to the death of my father. I will take leave of you now."

"What you say is perfectly reasonable," the King said in agreement. "It is important sometimes to look for meanings in events. Indeed sometimes it is all we have."

IV

Mauricio

When it was said that Emilio had had Mauricio adopted as soon as he won custody of the children at the time of his separation with Constancia, it was not adoption in the strict sense of the word, the type of adoption where an infant is left in a foundling wheel, or placed with a family through the services of an agency.

In fact Emilio had found a home for Mauricio through much simpler means, one that dispensed with any such formalities. It was his cook, Mia, who suggested the baby be given to her sister-in-law, who had just lost a child, said to be from cot death but in all likelihood from a case of cholera, a disease not unknown in the neighbourhood of Villa Fiorito in which she lived.

• • •

This woman, who was known as Silvia, doted on the illegitimate son of Lord Embers, notwithstanding the fact that the young boy always seemed to be in trouble. Possibly this was as much to do with the area in which they lived, as Villa Fiorito was the poorest of poor neighbourhoods, the type of place where you needed to walk to collect water from a hand pump: the type of place, in other words, where young men grow up fast. Mauricio's first brush with the law – the burglary of a laundry in downtown Buenos Aires – had resulted not in a prison sentence, but in a sound beating from the police. He had been almost proud of the welts he showed his mother.

"Mauricio, light of my life, the font from which I drink, how is it that you have grown up so bad?"

"Silvia," he replied (for he never called his adoptive mother "Mama"), "life is short and sweet. That wouldn't be so bad if it wasn't also unjust. I do not intend to sit back and watch others feast from the table. No, you will not see me eating crumbs."

Silvia's cousin on her mother's side, Morena, managed a small hostel in Recoleta, an area popular with back-packers. One day Silvia called on her with the view of trying to find Mauricio gainful employment there.

"He's a good sort, always willing to please," she told her cousin. "He has been in trouble with the police; but who from my barrio hasn't? All I'm asking is that you give him a second chance."

"A second chance?"

"If you can't help I'm not sure what I will do."

And so Morena gave Mauricio the job of night watchman. This involved manning the Reception area through the night, checking-in guests who arrived in the small hours, and generally keeping an eye on the smooth running of the place.

• • •

One night an altercation broke out in the street in front of the hostel between a young man and his travelling companion, a beautiful young woman. The young man was trying to coerce the young woman into the hostel lobby, pulling her by the wrist so forcefully her pale flesh was the colour of an oyster shell. Mauricio wasted no time in coming to her rescue.

"I'm giving you fair warning: if you don't stop what you're doing immediately," he told the gringo, "I shall intervene."

"Fuck off, asshole," the other replied.

"Don't say I didn't warn you."

And with one punch Mauricio laid the traveller flat out on the pavement. Taking the young lady carefully by the hand, he seated her in the reception area. She was the most beautiful woman he had ever seen: her smile, so simple and yet so complicated, was like a blossom; and her eyes were the deepest chestnut brown, the colour of the most luxurious leather.

"What is your name?" he asked her.

"Arabella," she replied.

• • •

The following morning Arabella came to thank Mauricio properly. They drank freshly squeezed pomegranate juice in a cáfe overlooking one of the city's grandest boulevards.

"This is not a country for a young woman to be travelling on her own," Mauricio cautioned her.

Arabella gave a coquettish smile. In truth she had been impressed by the way Mauricio had handled himself the previous night. "So what do you suggest I do?" she asked him.

"I suggest you permit me to accompany you."

And so Mauricio and Arabella made plans to go on together. They would travel to Patagonia, she told him. She had spent some time researching her family's genealogy; there were many settlers from Wales in Tierra del Fuego with whom she shared a surname.

"After that I will return home alone," she finished.

"And I shall be left with a broken heart," Mauricio tried to make light.

"Life is to be lived not sitting down but standing up," she reminded him.

"What you say is true," he agreed with her.

• • •

On the eve of their departure, Arabella had the strangest dream. She dreamt she was eating one of the most delicious apples she had ever tasted: not too sweet, not too tart, with flesh whiter than snow, edged pink where its immaculate skin had cast a glow. Until, suddenly, she saw that it was stained properly red. At first she kept on eating: nothing would stop her from tasting this flesh and savouring its juice. But once she realised it was her mouth that was bleeding, she could eat no more. She awoke, perplexed. Drinking another's blood might be repugnant, taboo even. But why should one baulk at tasting one's own, she wondered?

• • •

In order to travel with Arabella, Mauricio would need some money. So he approached an accomplice for a loan. It was a dark night, the type where the stars appear to be pinpricks in velvet. He found the accomplice in a local bar. Wild music was playing; dogs were barking. The air was full of tobacco smoke.

"This woman, she is English?" the accomplice asked Mauricio.

"She is from London."

"And she is beautiful?"

"Like no other."

"And how will I know you will not squander my money, and then be unable to repay it?"

"My friend, the opposite is the case. This young woman is well-born and well-connected. I intend not only to love her, but to use her to help me find my father."

"Not stories of your father again!" the accomplice sighed, throwing his glowing cigarette into the gutter.

"You will not laugh when you see my name in print."

"Remind me again who your father is?"

"His name is Lord Embers and he is godson of the King of England."

• • •

In truth Mauricio did not know for sure who his father was. It was all hearsay. It seems that his adoptive mother had made a promise on death not to reveal the names of Emilio and Constancia – however, no such promise was made about his foreign provenance. Indeed, Silvia would often call Mauricio "My little Lord Embers."

• • •

Mauricio waited until they were in Patagonia before he brought up the subject of his birth father. They were by the sea. It was too cold to swim, but blistering hot beneath a full sun. The beach was deserted, save for two women in black who were picking mussels from rocks recently revealed by the ebbing tide.

"There you have my story. In Argentina it is not something to be proud of to admit one is illegitimate," he sighed. "But with you I have bared my soul. Why? For two reasons. The first being that I love you. The second being that I wish you to help me."

Arabella had listened in polite silence. Also for two reasons. The first was that she had come to South America for adventure, not love. The second was that she knew the name of Lord Embers. In fact, he was a well-known figure in London society.

"You're sure he is your father?" she questioned him.

"Quite sure. And there is one other thing I know about him."

"And that is?"

"That he is the King of England's godson."

"I don't see how I can assist you. You will have to make your own enquiries," Arabella told Mauricio.

"But, my love . . ."

"Please do not call me that."

• • •

And at the first opportunity, Arabella abandoned Mauricio.

On checking into Santiago's *Marriot Hotel*, which they reached the following afternoon, she went out alone with a knapsack, on the pretext of needing to purchase some items from the pharmacy. In vain Mauricio waited for her that evening. Until at a presumably pre-arranged hour the concierge presented him with an envelope containing $200 in cash and a short note to explain that the hotel was paid up for four nights, to include all meals and drinks at the bar. The terse note offered no form of apology to soften the blow.

Mauricio sat at the bar whilst a pianist in black tie went through his dismal repertoire. It seemed this betrayal had made him only more determined than ever to find his father. These people who lived in Europe: they knew nothing of the struggle of life. If it fell to him, a simple man from the barrios, to teach them a lesson, then so be it.

• • •

The accomplice was scornful when Mauricio approached him for a second loan later that week. He was drinking in the same cantina. This time it was daylight. He had a kitten on his lap.

"You went where?" he asked Mauricio.

"To Patagonia."

"Because she had the same surname as settlers there?"

"That's what she said."

The accomplice's vulgar laugh revealed yellow teeth and blackened gums. It was a sight that disgusted Mauricio, yet he continued.

"If you don't lend me the money to reach England then I shall stow away on an airplane, climb into the landing gear of an Airbus and hope for the best. If I arrive it will be God's will."

"You shall freeze to death like every other fool who tries to cross the Atlantic that way."

"Then loan me the money."

"I will only loan it to you if you give me half of what you reap in your endeavours."

"Half is too much."

"Half of something is better than half of nothing."

And so Mauricio took the $2000 dollars that the accomplice pulled from his front trouser pocket, signing a simple contract the latter had drawn up on the back of a lottery ticket.

Back In London

Back in London Arabella mentioned her holiday romance to a friend, Maud Menzies. They were sitting beside the Round Pond in Kensington Gardens. A child had launched a boat into the centre of the pond, and was standing there at the water's edge, clearly puzzled as to how it could be retrieved.

"And do you know what he claimed?" Arabella finished. "That he was the illegitimate child of one of the King's godsons."

"The King has so many godchildren. Which one?"

"Lord Embers."

Lord Embers, as has been mentioned, was a well-known figure in London society. A talented architect, he had had a hand in some of the most impressive buildings new on the skyline.

"You don't mean Robert Embers?"

"You know him, don't you?"

"As a matter of fact I do."

"Do you think he should be informed?"

"Without any question."

• • •

Maud arranged to meet Lord Embers the following day for lunch at a fish restaurant overlooking Green Park. It was the height of summer and they were both wearing white. Maud waited until the bottle of wine they had ordered was all but finished before broaching the subject.

It was almost as if Lord Embers had known what was coming. No sooner had she embarked on her tale of Buenos Aires and Arabella's chance encounter with a handsome young man, than he put both hands to his temples, like a boxer preparing to protect himself from a flurry of punches.

"I am sorry to be the messenger," she finished.

"I shall not shoot you," the other tried to joke.

"It's true then?"

"In truth I have been waiting for this moment for some time," he told Maud Menzies.

• • •

Around this time the King had the most upsetting dream. One so strange it was difficult to recount, even to himself.

Basically it went something like this. In the gardens of Buckingham Palace there was a summerhouse in the gingerbread style. To one side of its decoratively ornate porch there was a heavy cover of ivy or some such and here, in this cover, a pair of exotic birds had nested to raise a brood. They were unlike any other bird the King had ever seen before, with tails even longer and more colourful than a bird of paradise's. In fact their tails were so long it seemed the fledglings, in returning to their nest, had to fly upside down for the last few feet in order to gain access to it.

The upsetting part of the dream was that there was a cat waiting beneath the nest, although it was possible it hadn't seen birds of this type before either, as it seemed perplexed and transfixed as it waited there, appearing to stand on its back legs as it rested on the trellis. The birds – there were three fledglings in and about the nest's entrance – most definitely hadn't seen a cat before, as they appeared to take no alarm. Indeed there followed long moments of stillness as prey and predator seemed in some manner to be in perfect harmony. Until, finally, the cat reached up and, in a gesture that could have been mistaken for affection, put a bent paw around one of the bird's necks.

Then, all of a sudden, the cat knew what it was about, and a desperate struggle ensued. A struggle which, naturally enough, was concluded in a most predictable fashion.

At this the King awoke. For some minutes he lay there, breathing hard. He was an older man by now and these types of dreams affected him to the core.

"Big Ben, Big Ben," he called out.

Big Ben had been in the habit of sleeping in an antechamber adjoining the King's bedroom for some time on account of the dreams that assailed the Sovereign. So this was nothing unusual to him. He rose as fast as he could, which wasn't as fast as all that given that he was, by now, an older man, too.

"I've had the most ghastly dream," the King told him.

"What was it, Your Highness?" Big Ben patiently asked.

"Beautiful birds . . . preyed on by a cat. I wonder what it can mean?"

"Not all dreams have to have a meaning," Big Ben tried to reassure the other.

"You always say that."

"Only because I think it's true."

"But what about the dream I had earlier this week about Lord Embers?"

"The one where he was in danger?"

"I suppose you think that was meaningless, too?"

• • •

Some days passed and still the King could not be free of the dream he had had of those exotic birds and the cat.

Finally, he decided he would instruct Big Ben to find Lord Embers. He had gone to sit in the gingerbread-style summerhouse in the palace gardens, as if by sitting there he might be able to dispel the menace that had pervaded the place in his sleep. He was wearing a thick dressing gown in spite of the warm weather and was seated with his back to the lake.

"Find Lord Embers and bring him here," he told Big Ben.

"Very good, Your Highness."

• • •

As Lord Embers was a well-known figure across London it wasn't difficult to track him down. Thinking a direct approach would be better than trying to reach him by telephone, Big Ben went straight to his headquarters, an imposing building off Tottenham Court Road.

He was ushered into an elliptical-shaped room with a conference table of rosewood, and waited for some minutes by the window, where traffic streamed silently below. Finally Lord Embers made his entrance, which he did by a second door.

"The King would like to see you," Big Ben came straight to the point.

Lord Embers looked flustered. He hadn't heard from the King for some time. Coming so close on his lunch with Maud Menzies he was convinced this summons must be in connection with the news that so weighed him down.

"He does?"

"See if you can't come this evening, His Highness is most anxious to see you."

• • •

Before he went to the palace, Lord Embers called on his mother, something he did every other evening. Lady Embers was now in her early eighties and had not left her bed in a year. The medication she was prescribed made her almost delirious.

"I am on my way to the palace," Lord Embers told her.

"But don't you live at the palace?" his mother returned.

"You know I don't, Mother. I live in Hammersmith."

"Tell your father to come home at once!" Lady Embers then said.

"Mother, Father has been dead for more than thirty years, you know that."

"Dead? How so?"

"He died in a fishing accident."

"A *fishing* accident! I've never heard of anything so preposterous! Tell him to come home at once. I have a gold sovereign I must give him."

At the mention of the gold sovereign, Lord Embers' demeanour darkened.

"Why must you give it to him?" he asked his mother.

"Because it's the most fearfully bad luck. All the King's sovereigns are a curse. I want your Father to take the sovereign and give it back to the King."

And at this, her hair wild, her eyes even more so, she tried to haul herself up in bed.

"Okay, okay, I'll tell him to come home," Lord Embers tried to placate his mother.

"He *is* alive, then? Why do you lie to me so?"

"Because he is both alive and not alive."

At this Lady Embers descended into gales of laughter.

• • •

Lord Embers found the King in the nursery, where the Sovereign was making an inspection of his birds' egg collection.

"Lord Embers, thank heavens you've come."

"What is it, Your Majesty?" the other tremulously asked.

"Lord Embers, do you ever dream?"

"Seldom, but when I do I often find it quite unsettling."

"Me, too. But tell me, how are you?"

"My business is flourishing and I have a young family."

"A son, I understand?"

"One, Sir."

"And his name?"

"Felix, Sir."

The King seemed reassured. "So nothing's amiss?"

How Lord Embers would have liked to unburden himself! "Not that I know of," he replied.

"That *is* a relief to me. You see, I was convinced something wasn't . . . how can I put it: quite right?"

"It is good of you to take such an interest in me, Your Highness."

"But how could I not when you are my godson, a godson who lost his own father in such tragic circumstances?"

"That was a long time ago, Sir."

"To me it could have happened just yesterday. I suspect we shall all discover sooner or later that time is perfectly meaningless when it comes to matters of that sort."

Cal's Fare

Of all the characters encountered to date, it was perhaps Cal – the kind man whom Kai had encountered all those years ago at a meeting of *Gamblers Anonymous* – who had been most favoured by fate. There had been setbacks, naturally – an acrimonious divorce and medical problems, too – but for the main he had been at peace. He now lived alone in north London's Camden Town, on the top floor of a double-fronted house with extensive views over the capital, a capital amongst whose streets he had been driving a black cab for nigh on half a century now.

Every dozen years or so Cal would return to his birthplace, the Caribbean island of St Vincent. There he would lie beneath the tropical sun, the trade winds clacking and glistening in the palms, and pray to the god of his understanding, expressing sentiments of humility and gratitude. It didn't trouble him that each time he visited the island there were fewer relatives to call upon. For that was the way with life.

This serenity had everything to do with maintaining his sobriety from the menace of gambling. The days when his hands were inky from the newsprint of racing cards were but a dim memory, as threadbare as a dream. In fact by now he was one of the capital's most respected members of *Gamblers Anonymous*, regularly representing his local group at conference level.

On account of his sobriety, Cal had long ago accrued sufficient savings on which to retire. Yet he continued to work. What he treasured most was the sense of journey, of each day having a new beginning, and the fact that no two days were ever the same. He may no longer have frequented the betting shops, but he welcomed this element of mystery in his work, seeing magic in the potential of the maze that confronted him each morning, imbued as it was with an aura of chance.

• • •

One evening – a few days after Lord Embers' interview with his godfather at the palace – Cal picked up a fare from Heathrow Airport, a young man with thick black hair and a tattoo on his neck. The fact that this young man was travelling so light – he had only a small weather-beaten rucksack – made Cal a little wary, as over his long career he had had more incidents than he cared to remember of punters absconding without paying their dues.

"Where to?" he asked.

"St James's."

"Where in St James's?"

"Just take me to Admiralty Arch."

And before Cal could make a proper decision as to

whether or not to take this fare, the young man was seated in the back of his cab.

"Come far?" Cal quizzed him as they joined the motorway into the capital.

"Buenos Aires."

"Here for holidays?"

"Not exactly."

"Family business, then?"

"You could call it that," the other replied, sinking into his seat and so firmly but politely precluding any further exchange.

Presently they arrived at their destination, where Cal had a better opportunity to scrutinize the visitor from overseas. Not only did the young man have a winning smile and dark, thoughtful eyes, he also turned out to be a generous tipper.

"Why, thank you!" Cal said, accepting a $10 bill.

"You're welcome."

"Enjoy your visit to our capital."

"Don't worry, I shall."

How often it was in life that one was reminded to keep an open mind, Cal thought to himself as he pulled away from the kerb. And yet there was something about this fellow, he sensed, that didn't altogether add up.

• • •

Mauricio – for this had been Cal's fare – had no intention of paying for a room in a hotel or hostel. Instead, he headed straight for St James's Park, where in a bank of rhododendrons he created a make-shift camp for the night, hanging all his clothes from branches, which, arranged in this fashion, resembled magic lanterns.

Owing to the time difference, he found he was not in the least tired. So he decided to take a walk. His first impressions of London were favourable. The pavements were clean and the air clear, a big improvement on Buenos Aires. For some time he stood outside the gates of Buckingham Palace, staring up at the honeycomb windows; then he headed northwest, following the perimeter of the palace's boundary wall. But no sooner was he half way along than suddenly there was a smash accompanied by the sound of breaking glass. Simultaneously a number of the street lamps, old-fashioned street lamps at that, were extinguished. A car passed him and stopped some distance ahead. Followed by another, and then a third.

If Mauricio hadn't been from the barrios he probably would have retraced his steps; but danger wasn't something he had learnt to avoid. Quite the opposite, in fact, and shortly he was within hailing distance of a gang of men who seemed to be assembling a ladder with which they were going to scale the palace's wall.

"Who the fuck are you?" one of them cursed.

"My name's Mauricio and I've just arrived from Buenos Aires," Mauricio replied.

"Get lost," another growled in a threatening manner, and was about to advance on Mauricio when there came a piercing wolf-whistle from the top of the road. At this the robbers scattered, some disappearing into the darkness of the park, others regaining the cars in which they had arrived. To Mauricio all this could have been a dream, and for a moment he was left quite alone, as if encased in a tomb of glassy silence.

Then there was the sound of someone shouting through a megaphone.

"Put down your weapon and hands up!"

"I don't have a weapon."

"Hands up, I said!"

• • •

At the police station Mauricio's story was received with great mirth. In fact many more than the permitted number of officers than were allowed had crammed themselves into the interview room in order to bear witness to the young man's statement.

"So, Mauricio Jesus Gonzalez, to recap: you're from the barrios of Buenos Aires, your father is called Lord Embers and you thought you'd sleep in St James's Park because the King is your father's godfather," the sergeant in charge asked Mauricio to confirm.

"That is correct, sir."

"So perhaps you could explain why, seeing as you're so closely related to the King's godson, you should need to break into the palace."

"But I wasn't breaking in."

"Then why were you standing at the foot of a rope ladder?"

At this Mauricio could offer no explanation.

"Take him to the cells."

• • •

There was one officer there, however, who wore a deepening frown, since the whole evening had given him a distinct sense of déjà vu. For a moment he wondered if he weren't seeing things.

"That's the strangest thing," he said to a colleague as Mauricio was taken down to the cells.

"What's that?" the other asked.

"About twenty years ago – I was a bobby on the beat then, you understand – I arrested a young man in Tooting . . . and he, too, said exactly the same thing."

"Oh, yes?"

"Well, not exactly the same thing. But he said he was Lord Embers and that he also was the King's godson."

• • •

This police officer, whose name was Simpson, didn't want to look a fool; nor did he wish to withhold information, however implausible, that might be of benefit to the nation. In the end he decided it was only right to warn the King. So he contacted Big Ben through the usual channels.

"I agree, that is rather strange," Big Ben agreed with Simpson once he had heard him out.

"I thought it only proper to let you know."

"You did right. You see, the King dreamt about Lord Embers only last week."

"He did?"

"Our Sovereign puts great store by his reveries. Not that he can remember much about this particular one. Only that it was a clear warning."

"I see."

"And now you've come here this morning with this 'intelligence' . . . Well, even the most sceptical of doubters might have reason to carefully consider their position with regard to the dream world."

"Quite so."

Together the two men discussed what should be done regarding extra security for the palace; and it was settled that two specialist officers should be detailed to patrol the grounds until further notice.

"I shall let the King know you have been to see me this morning. He will wish me to thank you on his behalf, which I am doing now."

• • •

When the King heard of this he nodded wisely.

"What you tell me doesn't surprise me in the least. What more is known about this Mauricio?"

"All we know is that he's from the barrios, Sir."

"We're quite sure he's Lord Embers' illegitimate son, though?"

The King did not have to listen to the answer – which involved a cook, her sister-in-law and a neighbourhood in Buenos Aires called Villa Fiorito – he was wondering instead what should be done under the circumstances.

"I mean, do you think we ought to warn Lord Embers?" he asked when Big Ben had finished.

"I'm not sure, Sir. What do you think?"

"I'm of the opinion this fellow from the barrios isn't seeking to make contact with Lord Embers in order to enjoy a familial relationship per se. I think he has pecuniary gain foremost in his sights."

"What you say is quite possible, Sir."

"That being the case, perhaps it would be better if we *did* intervene. Find this fellow and pay him off with a proper contract, a contract which would prevent him from ever entering the Kingdom again."

"Are you sure that's wise, Sir? Don't you remember all that trouble we had with Parker-Jarvis?"

"That was quite different. And, anyway, nothing too dire came of all that in the end, if my memory serves me correctly. I don't know, Big Ben. I wish I did, but I just *don't*. And not knowing is making me feel exhausted. Perhaps tomorrow I will know."

• • •

But the following morning, even after two turns around the lake, the King was no clearer.

"Are you sure it's wise to become so involved?" Big Ben tried to counsel his Sovereign again.

"I feel entirely involved already, Big Ben. Lord Embers' father died whilst I was fishing *Otter's Hole*, and all because of a wager. Then I sent the young man to a ranch in Argentina, and so implicated myself further in the matter of his destiny. The present Lord Embers is a successful man, but could well be outdone by this fellow from the barrios. He could be a thorn in his side from this day forward. I think we are beholden to make terms with this rascal – he is only after money, after all – and so save Lord Embers, whom I have only imperilled. Big Ben, bring me the sovereigns."

"But you haven't used the sovereigns for years, Your Highness."

"This isn't a matter for us. A sovereign must decide it."

Big Ben was right: the gold sovereigns had not been used for a dozen years or more. A collection of them had remained untouched in a drawer of a bureau in the King's dressing room.

"**HEADS** we warn Lord Embers and do no more, **TAILS** we say nothing to Lord Embers and make our own arrangements."

"Right you are, Sir."

The King tossed the coin, which spun and flashed in the air before rolling under the piano. Big Ben had to go down on all fours to determine the verdict.

"It's **TAILS**, Sir."

"You're quite sure?"

"Quite sure, Sir."

• • •

The first thing Mauricio did on being released by the police was to return to his makeshift camp in St James's Park. There he found his possessions, each and every one of them, turned over or missing.

He sat on a tree stump, surveying the mess. How foolish he felt! Here he was, a man from the barrios, well versed in the affairs of men: how was it possible he had allowed himself to be arrested within a matter of hours of landing at Heathrow Airport? And to lose all his personal effects to boot?

Presently there was the sound of someone pushing their way into the camp through the branches. It was a young woman. She wore a waxed coat that stretched nearly to her knees and a deerstalker hat.

"And who are you?" Mauricio challenged her.

"Bowen's the name."

"See here, Bowen, my possessions which I left here in good faith whilst I went for a walk and then was subsequently wrongly detained by the constabulary, have been trashed one and all. Perhaps it is you who is the culprit?"

"Not me, my friend, but I did witness a group of homeless men rooting through your effects."

"There was not much of value in any case," Mauricio sighed, "but I can see that I shall have to pay more attention in future. This place is as bad as the barrios."

"And where exactly are the barrios, if I may be so bold as to ask?"

And so Mauricio and Bowen struck up a friendship. Bowen, who was a little older than Mauricio, liked the young man's fresh, healthy-looking face and his indomitable spirit. Mauricio, for his part, quite fancied this girl in her coat of wax with her honey-coloured hair and scarlet lipstick. He would like to have run his hand down her back to feel the way she moved beneath his touch.

"How did you get here from South America?" she asked him.

"Being impervious to cold, I travelled here in the undercarriage of an aircraft," the other answered.

"If you are so hot-blooded you have come to the wrong place," Bowen told him.

"You think so?"

"Unless, of course, there is a specific reason why you're here?"

"In fact I am here to settle some debts."

"And what debts might they be?"

When Mauricio did not answer, she added coyly: "I only ask as more often than not debt collectors require assistants."

• • •

About a week later Cal was at a meeting of *Gamblers Anonymous*, when he had a surprise.

The meeting, which was held in the crypt of a church, was larger than usual and, being a little late, there was only room to sit at the back. With his eyes closed – for this was the way he liked best to relax – he had to listen carefully as the speaker, who was a visitor from the USA, began to recount his story.

"For many years now I have been free of the compulsion to gamble. In fact tomorrow it will be twenty years since I took my last wager," this man began.

Applause.

"But never have I felt so bereft and alone as I do today. In fact you could almost say that today I have lost pretty much everything," the speaker went on to a silenced auditorium. "Only, of course, as everyone here will have come to appreciate, it is not loss and gain which is at the heart of our condition."

The stranger's story was harrowing. He had lost his wife to cancer the previous autumn – on Thanksgiving Day, no less. And no sooner was she buried in a remote cemetery in northern California, than he had lost his house as well. Not forfeited in circumstances familiar to those assembled, rather by natural causes: there had been a devastating earthquake, which had caused a fire in the valley.

"Being unable to insure our properties against this risk, most of us in the community have lost everything," he explained.

Cal was by now on the edge of his seat, straining to see the speaker better. It couldn't be the Californian he had met all those years ago, could it? Yes it was! The man was greyer about the temples and seemed a little smaller in stature, his hands more sinewy at any rate . . . but there he was!

As soon as the meeting was over, Cal approached him.

"Kai!"

"It's grand to see you again, Cal!"

"It is incredible, no?"

"We are members of an extraordinary fellowship, are we not?"

They went to the same café overlooking the canal. And for old time's sake even ate the same dish of pasta with tomato sauce.

"I am glad life has been kind to you, Cal," Kai smiled at his old friend once they had traded stories.

"And I am sorry for your losses," the other replied.

"Who said there was no such thing as bad luck, eh?"

"Some fool, I suspect! But do you know the most extraordinary thing happened just the other night?" Cal leaned in.

"What was that?"

And so Cal explained how the previous week he had picked up a fare from the airport, a young man who claimed to be the son of the King of England's godson.

"You don't mean Lord Embers?" Kai frowned. "It can't be true!"

"I dropped him near Buckingham Palace, where later that night he tried to scale the walls into the palace's gardens. The papers have been full of it."

Kai looked thoughtful. "Don't you think it's strange, Cal, that this Lord Embers business should feature in the way it does in our friendship?" he said. "Like a kernel or a piece of grit in an oyster, it is the common denominator of something beyond and outside of us."

"Isn't that rather fanciful?"

"Perhaps it is. But don't you think it's strange that each time we meet there is something of this Embers business?"

"As a matter of fact I do."

"What do you think it means?"

"I couldn't tell you. I could only say I don't find it altogether unwelcome," the other returned.

The King's Plan

It was indeed fortunate for Mauricio that he had fallen in with Bowen. Without her guidance he might well have struggled in this strange capital. Most likely he would have been detained a second time in as many days.

"Smash and grab has no place here, Bandito," she told him as they took the escalator down to the platforms at Embankment's underground station. "Watch me carefully and learn. We will move through the train together, and when you see me rub my fingers like this," and here she made a testing for oil gesture between her thumb and forefinger, "then and only then do you make a move."

Bowen was right: there were many more cameras in London than in Buenos Aires. Indeed you could almost say the place was alive with hidden eyes. They did a trial run first, moving in single file through the swaying carriages, squeezing past those who stood reaching up to steady themselves, briefcases clamped between their ankles. Bowen had taken off her deerstalker and had pushed up her hair. She hadn't applied any more rouge; rather it was her eyes that she darkened with kohl. Making that universal gesture with thumb and forefinger, she would stop when she saw potential in an unsuspecting passenger, and would wait for Mauricio to take up position, from where he could casually assess the situation.

Then, at Oxford Circus, they changed to the Victoria Line and began in earnest. By 4 o'clock that afternoon they had £2,200 between them in cash.

• • •

That evening they took a room in a hotel in Bayswater. Now was the time for their lovemaking. Mauricio's fingers, like ballet dancers on a tabletop, explored Bowen's vertebrae and her slender hips. How good it was to hear her moan when he teased her nipples between his young lips, gently pulling at them, like water draining over sand.

"Why do you wish to exact revenge on this young woman?" Bowen asked him as they lay apart at last. "You know these sentiments of bitterness only harden the arteries."

"In our country we always settle our debts. Not to do so would mean you are as good as half way to the grave."

"She touched you, then, this gringa?"

"She disrespected me."

"And the other debt you wish to settle? Tell me about that."

"Now is not the moment."

"Why not?"

"What is romance without mystery?"

• • •

Little did they know it, but the Prendice brothers, the King's detectives, had been monitoring their every move. The next morning these brothers followed Mauricio and Bowen to Marble Arch, where it was clear the young lovers intended to embark on a second day of crime.

The brothers were dressed identically, in pinstripe suits and bowler hats, although they differed in height. It was Ernest, the older and taller of the two, who put himself in the line of fire, so to speak, by pretending to concentrate on a crossword puzzle as the train thundered through its interminable tunnels of darkness.

• • •

At lunch the lovers took stock in a café in Islington.

"A good morning's work, Bandito," Bowen praised her protégé, "but what to do with these?" she frowned, spilling a handful of gold sovereigns from a velvet purse over the tabletop between them. "From whom did you rob these?"

"From the man with the umbrella," Mauricio answered, squeezing her thigh.

"I wasn't sure about the man with the umbrella," Bowen muttered, her frown deepening, "and now we have his gold. Get off me, you fool!"

The only person Bowen knew who might have a view about these gold sovereigns was a receiver of stolen goods in Limehouse, a fence who went by the name of PJ. Parker-Jarvis had not weathered well: he had only a few teeth left and was missing the lobe of one ear.

"These are most unusual," he said, putting away his eyepiece. "Pray, how did you come by them?"

"We found them in a purse in a discarded briefcase."

"Is that a fact?"

"In Regent Street."

PJ nodded nonchalantly. He was anything but nonchalant, however. He had recognized these sovereigns the moment they had been tipped from their purse.

"In a discarded briefcase, you say?" he repeated.

"In a manner of speaking," Bowen answered.

"Do you know I think they are most unusual?"

Business was not conducted like this in Buenos Aires, and Mauricio was growing impatient. "Gold is gold," he said, "and if you do not wish to purchase these sovereigns from us then we will have no alternative but to offer them to someone else."

"And where do you hail from?" PJ asked, looking at Mauricio properly for the first time.

"From the barrios of Buenos Aires," the other answered, scooping the coins back into the purse and standing, "a place where business is transacted with a little more verve than it is here beside your sluggish Thames."

"My advice to you is to have these melted down as soon as possible," PJ said, standing, too.

"That's good advice," Mauricio proudly answered.

• • •

But no sooner had they reached the top of the street than the Prendice brothers stepped forward to apprehend them.

"We have been monitoring your activities all morning," the younger of the two, who went by the name of Milo, informed the criminals, "and now you have stepped out of a public house acquainted by those receiving stolen goods. You can come quietly or otherwise, the choice is entirely yours."

"You do not look like policemen, show us your ID," Bowen demanded.

"You are right, we are not policemen, we are Special Forces attached to the palace, and it is there we shall be taking you."

"Whether you like it or not," Ernest added.

• • •

And so an hour later the two villains found themselves before the King. Ernest summed up the case against them.

"We had been observing them all morning, Your Highness, and we laid a trap. These gold sovereigns you see before you now," he said, spilling the heap of gold on the table behind which the King was sitting, "were in this pouch in my jacket pocket. On finding them missing, we followed the miscreants to a well-known public house in Limehouse, where unquestionably they were trying to dispose of them."

"Now, you look here, you two," the King began in his sternest manner, "you are both guilty of a most heinous crime. These sovereigns belonged to my late grandmother, they formed part of her dowry. If you had managed to dispose of them in the manner I imagine you sought, these beautiful coins may well have been melted down by now and their stamp lost for all time. I am asking you to be clear from the outset. How do you intend to plead to the charges of this crime?"

Bowen was about to answer, when Mauricio silenced her with a wave of his hand.

"We would like to plead guilty, but by way of mitigation I would like it to be taken into account that I, myself, was robbed," he answered.

"*You* were robbed?"

"And unjustly treated. I had no sooner arrived in this city of yours, than I, too, was relieved of most of what I owned, and then, to add insult to injury, thrown into jail. If you will let me explain?"

"Go on," the King waved.

And so Mauricio outlined his position. Not only had he lost all his worldly goods in St James's Park, he had been arrested not a stone's throw from where they were standing now, wrongly suspected and accused of trying to scale the palace's perimeter wall. And this had all happened within two hours of arriving in the capital!

"So it was you who was apprehended at the foot of a rope ladder?" the King cunningly put it.

"But I had a reason to be here," Mauricio then said.

"And pray, what is that?'

"I may be from the barrios, but I am of noble birth. You see, my father is, in fact, a man well known to you."

"And who might that be?"

"Lord Embers, your godson, no less."

The King rather liked Mauricio's direct manner. Indeed there was something distinctly refreshing in the way he was so offhand and confident.

"I can see that we shall have to speak man to man," he nodded sagely. "In truth we had had intelligence of your impending arrival here in the city. And had been waiting for you," the King added.

Mauricio's eyes narrowed. "I think I know to whom you are referring in terms of this informant," he said. "Naturally I'd be very interested to know what someone of that character has chosen to say about me. You are aware of the nature of our encounter, I presume?"

"In part."

"Well, perhaps you will permit me to acquaint you with the full facts? One balmy evening in downtown Buenos Aires I rescued a young woman who was suffering at the hands of a compatriot. She was only too happy to be escorted to Tierra del Fuego, a place of few people and vast scenery, where she told me some of her ancestors had emigrated. Only when I laid before her my own situation and suggested how she might assist me, then do you know what happened? No? Well, it was this way. Instead of speaking face to face like we are doing now, this person chose to vanish, return to the United Kingdom without so much as a 'Hasta la vista'. Further, she sought to add insult to injury by asking another, a hotel concierge no less, to pay me off."

"Well, that is rather shoddy," the King admitted. "But perhaps you would like to explain how you imagined this subject of mine could have assisted you?"

"Doesn't everyone need to know from whence they hail?" was the answer, plainly put.

"Yes and no," the King carefully replied.

"Yes and no?"

"Naturally as Sovereign I have often wondered about the phenomenon 'accident of birth'. Everything you see here," he waved a hand over the interior of the room, "and a great deal more besides – all this bestowed upon me by chance. Yet, of course, I am no more than the titular owner of these earthly chattels, a steward, no less."

"It is interesting to hear you refer to the phenomenon 'accident of birth'," Mauricio said with a wry smile and a gentle wave of his own, "as it is something about which I have given some thought myself. But what, may I ask, are you suggesting?"

"I am suggesting that we are no more than stewards of our own selves, too. That it is immaterial from whence we hove. Let us consider your friend in Tierra del Fuego. Don't tell me she felt any better for seeing the vast valleys and snow-capped peaks just because her ancestors had crossed the Atlantic to reach them."

The King had a point, Mauricio had to concede. Arabella hadn't seemed in the least moved by the scenery that dwarfed her. Or the simple people they had encountered on the roadside, crouched inside their ponchos.

"What is the nature of your profession, if you don't mind my asking?" the King went on.

"I am a supervisor in a factory," Mauricio lied.

"Doubtless you would like to own your own factory one day?"

"That is my ambition."

"Only perhaps you lack the wherewithal at present?"

Mauricio's English was not good enough to understand this.

"I mean to say perhaps you do not possess sufficient capital with which to launch such a venture," the King explained.

"And you will provide this capital?"

"Perhaps I do have a proposal. But first I should like to speak a little more about Lord Embers."

And so the King explained how the poor boy had grown up without a father, without even knowing his father on account of this man having died in a tragic accident; how the King had taken a special interest in him on account of that fact, personally paying the fees for his studies so that he could succeed in his ambition to become an architect. Lord Embers presently lived in a district in London called Hammersmith, a modest enough place, the King began to wind up. He had a wife and a son. He worked hard and was a dutiful husband.

"As you will doubtless appreciate, I have painted a picture of a most civilized man," the King concluded.

"Indeed."

"And now I come to the difficult part."

And the King began to outline the difficulties that might arise if Mauricio sought to become a feature in the life of his biological father. Difficulties for both of them. Indeed, wouldn't it be better if both tried to resume their lives as they had led them forthwith? In the knowledge that a father had a son and that a son had a father, but content alone in that knowledge without having to take any steps to alter the status quo?

"You would like me to return to the barrios?" Mauricio asked the King.

"This is where I can help."

"Go on."

"Put simply, I propose to set you up in business in your home country, but on strict condition."

"On condition that I desist in approaching my father, you mean?"

"I can see that we understand each other perfectly, Señor Gonzalez."

"You have taken your time in coming to the point," the other smiled, "when from the outset I could see where this was heading. It has given me time to consider my terms."

"Business is always best conducted briskly. Pray, name them and let us be detained no further in our negotiations."

"I shall return to Buenos Aires and once there surrender my passport which will mean I can never leave the country again. For that I would require a million pounds."

"A million pounds!" the King gasped.

"But I would also want something else."

"Something else?"

"I do not wish to meet my father. I agree with you: there will exist many difficulties in our future relationship, some of them unknown at this point. But I would wish to see him. And without him knowing that he has been seen."

"I don't understand," the King frowned.

"Have him in a restaurant, have him in the street, have him in a car waiting at a set of traffic lights – but let me pass him and let me look into my father's eyes. Let me see because, believe me, I would like to see this man."

• • •

That night Big Ben summoned Lord Embers to the palace, this time by telephone.

The King was in the nursery again. Some replacement tern eggs had been delivered from Sandringham that morning and he was personally overseeing the procedure of exchanging like for like, which included making a detailed entry in a leather-bound ledger.

"Robert, thank you for coming to see me," he began, closing the last of the cabinet's mahogany drawers.

"I think I know why you have summoned me again," Lord Embers answered. "In fact it was wrong of me not to have been more open with you the last time we met. You have asked me to visit you again this evening to discuss Mauricio Jesus Gonzalez, haven't you?"

"Thank you for your tact in so quickly coming to the point. And I shall come to the point with the same purpose and velocity. I have some news for you, Robert."

"You do?" the young Lord Embers anxiously asked.

"Whether it is good news or otherwise I will let you be the judge. At any rate, I hope you find it helpful."

And so the King related all that had been said in his meeting with Mauricio. With one crucial omission, however: there was no mention of the million pounds. There was talk of inducements in the shape of introductions the King might make on behalf of the young man – the King knew many businessmen in Latin America – but in the main it had been other considerations they had discussed, he said.

"Being a bright boy he's perfectly aware of the difficulties that would doubtless arise should your relationship be formalized. It would be wrong for me to take credit where credit is not due, but I think speaking all this through with a third party has made things clearer still in his mind. Mr. Gonzalez does have one *request*, however," the King finished, thinking request a better word than *condition*.

"Yes?"

"He wishes to see you, Robert, before he boards his airplane. He doesn't wish to speak to you, or for you to even know he's seen you. But he wants, to use the expression, to 'clap eyes on you'. Which perhaps, under the circumstances, is perfectly understandable, given he will go forward in future with that particular avenue closed to him. Now, how do you feel about that?"

"Well, first of all let me express my gratitude for the offer you have made this young man on my behalf," Lord Embers answered, clearly relieved by everything he had just heard.

"But now I need to ask you to reflect very carefully for a moment, Lord Embers," the King went on. "I need you to consider your own position. This young man from the barrios has asked me to orchestrate a situation in which he observes you without you being aware of being observed, as it were. That's all very well and good, but how do you feel about it? Of course I wouldn't arrange this without your knowledge or consent. It is not for me to write the score, it is more my task to conduct the orchestra."

"Do you mean do I want to see my own son?" Lord Embers asked.

"That is precisely what I mean."

"If I'm absolutely honest I was thinking exactly the same thing myself. That I *would* like to see my son . . . just the once . . . and then no more."

The King clasped his godson by the hand and gave him a firm handshake. "I have a feeling this may work out very well," he pronounced. "I did, in fact, anticipate your answer, or at least consider how we might proceed in the event of your answering in the manner you have. Would you like to hear what I thought?"

"Very much, Your Majesty, and thank you again."

"My thoughts were such: we summon Mauricio Jesus Gonzalez to the palace, and present him with a ticket for a flight leaving for Buenos Aires that very evening. He will then ask about the request he has made, and we shall tell him that you, Lord Embers, will be at the airport. In the lounge or at the bar, it's immaterial. He will then have the opportunity of observing you and then immediately afterwards boarding the plane."

"And how shall I see him, Sir?"

"You, Lord Embers, shall see him first at the palace. I shall summon him here on the pretext of giving a reception party in his honour. You will be in disguise, dressed up in your old uniform, just as if you were in attendance at a state function. Standing by the door or waiting table you will have ample opportunity to take stock of the situation and in your own time. How do you feel about that?"

"Well, I think it's brilliant, Your Highness."

"I rather thought so myself."

Nick Winter's Confession

Nick Winter had done well in his job with Mr. Richardson. So well, in fact, that he had been granted a lifetime interest in one of the estate's cottages, a simple bungalow of slate and stone.

If the gesture had been made in the spirit of reward, it had also been offered as an enticement to settle permanently. In this regard, it would have given Mr. Richardson some satisfaction to see his employee fettling the paintwork on the bungalow's sash windows and timber eaves each June. To witness the reclamation of the vegetable garden, which had fallen into such a state of disrepair at the hands of the previous tenant. To sample the honey from the ghillie's hives; and the copper-black Maran eggs that were brought to the Big House in times of plenty.

It couldn't be said that Nick was a popular man on the estate, however. Habitually eschewing the company of his fellow workers, he seldom attended the annual dinner of Thanksgiving his employer hosted at the Big House, for instance. More telling perhaps was the fact that his children, and his children's children, were rarely visitors at Gardener's Cottage, either. It wasn't so much that the ghillie was disliked, it was more his aloofness towards others which did him no favours.

It was therefore a surprise to all those who knew him – and those who didn't know him, besides – when Nick married for the second time. He had met his wife, Rosemary, in their local town of St Boswells, where she was assistant librarian. The daughter of a minister, she was single-minded and devout, without being pious, and admired Nick for his natural resilience and quiet confidence – but without properly knowing him, as it were. She was aware of the accident on the River Dee, but had only spoken of it once with her husband. Consequently when Nick became depressed at the prospect of retirement, she was perplexed.

"You will have more time for the garden. You could win prizes at the Show."

"Prizes at the Show," the other would mutter.

• • •

Then, one night, Nick had the most disturbing dream.

He dreamt he was away from home, but somehow had knowledge that his house was being ransacked. It didn't seem to concern him that his drawers and cupboards should be turned inside out and anything of value taken. What mattered more was that a strong box – a steel box he had never before seen in his waking life – should not be disturbed. Part of him believed that the box, being carefully hidden in the loft of an outbuilding, would be overlooked; another part of him knew it would be turned over, too, and its contents pillaged.

When he arrived at the house it couldn't be said that he

wasn't prepared for the worst. But what he found was shocking nonetheless: the place had the appearance of being looted by a retreating army. Nick raced to the outbuilding, more preoccupied than ever as to the fate of the strong box. He was right: it had not been overlooked. But what was strange was that its contents were perfectly preserved.

He awoke blowing hard.

"What's got into you?" his wife asked.

"I dreamt I was done for," the ghillie replied.

• • •

The following morning he phoned the palace and spoke to Big Ben.

Big Ben had always liked Nick Winter. "Winter, how are you? It's been a while, has it not?"

"I need to see the King," the other answered.

"It's urgent, then?"

"More urgent than I care to admit."

• • •

The King said he would be happy to see his faithful ghillie, so that night Nick took the sleeper train from Edinburgh, arriving in London's Kings Cross at 6.30 am the following morning. From there he walked the whole way to Buckingham Palace, rehearsing over and over again all that he was going to say.

The King was in the gingerbread house. He had set up his telescope to observe a pair of tufted ducks that had recently come to nest on the island. Big Ben ushered Nick into the folly's single room, which had windows either side of the door and a simple fireplace (non-functioning) to complete the illusion of habitation.

"Well, well, Mr. Winter," the King said offering his hand, "this is quite a surprise."

"It's good of you to see me, Your Highness," the other replied, bowing.

"I'll never know why you chose to leave us at Balmoral. Unless, of course, it was on account of that dreadful accident."

"It's that about which I need to speak, Sir."

"About the drowning of Lord Embers, you mean?"

"Yes, Sir."

"Then, pray, take a seat and tell me what's on your mind."

Once Big Ben had tactfully left the two alone, Nick began to speak. He may have rehearsed everything he wished to say on his way to the palace and the order in which he wished to say it, but now he found his tongue had a mind of its own.

"It was no accident, Sir. Lord Embers died at my hands. We were beyond the island and the neck of the pool . . . I brought the boat broadside into the stream . . . and because of that he went in. Granted, I looked for him . . . but he should never have been in the water in the first place."

"But Lord Embers was a large and clumsy man."

"Your Highness, I am responsible for the death of Lord Embers."

The King had great affection for his former ghillie. They had caught many fish together and, together, had weathered many disappointments.

"You're quite sure of this, Winter?" he asked.

"I wouldn't have come all this way and after so many years if I wasn't sure."

"But can I ask why you should feel at fault? I mean to say, did you have a particular grudge against Lord Embers? Speaking man to man, I know Lord Embers was an unpopular person, but had he done anything specifically to upset you?"

Nick Winter was determined to be honest. "He had removed a picture, Your Highness," he answered.

"A picture? Which picture?"

And so Nick described the waif-like figure – without describing her gossamer-thin shawl – that had hung, framed in lacquered wood, outside the rod room door at Balmoral.

"There was something about that picture, Sir. Every time I was at the castle, I looked out for it. Only that fateful morning it had been removed by Lord Embers, the reason being that he was offended by it and that others would find it offensive and indecent, too."

"But how extraordinary, I know the picture well!"

"You do?"

"And I remember well asking Lord Embers to remove it from its place beside the rod room door. For the simple reason that I wished to have it upstairs, somewhere where I could enjoy it properly myself."

"You mean you and not Lord Embers instructed its removal?"

"That's right, Winter."

For some time the two men sat in contemplative silence, until the sound of a coot skittering across the lake finally broke the spell.

"I must say this is most extraordinary," the King murmured.

"Do you think the police need to be involved, Sir?" Nick asked.

"Good heavens, no! Not after all these years."

"You don't think I should own up to this crime?"

"You've owned up to it to me, haven't you?"

And when Nick still looked unconvinced, the King put a hand on his shoulder and said: "Winter, you're to come with me."

• • •

And so the King took Nick Winter into the palace, and upstairs into his private sanctum. The picture of the waif-like girl in her gossamer-thin shawl was hanging to the right of the Sovereign's bed.

"It's yours, Winter," the King declared, handing the picture to his trusted ghillie.

"Your Majesty, I'm lost for words," the other returned.

"Take it away."

"You're quite sure I shouldn't go to the police?"

"Quite sure."

And when Nick still didn't look persuaded, the King had a good idea.

"I tell you what could settle this matter once and for all," he said.

"Yes?" the ghillie enquired.

"A toss of a coin. And I'll tell you why. For nigh on half a century I have blamed myself for the untimely death of Lord Embers, convinced it was owing to a bet we had taken on who would catch the best fish before lunch that had contributed to his demise. And now you have come to me with an equally tenuous proposition, that out of a sense of resentment at the loss of this simple picture, you guided the boat into unsuitable water, causing Lord Embers, who in any case was a large and clumsy man, to lose his footing and subsequently drown. Granted Lord Embers was an unpopular man and had removed the picture you are holding, but equally I was responsible in suggesting the wager. So we are both to 'blame', are we not?"

"In a fashion, Sir."

"As far as I can see it we either call the police this very instant and explain to them the new evidence you have brought this morning – a quasi confession of sorts – or you leave your secret with me, the fall of a coin once and for all putting this matter to rest."

The King could see that Nick Winter was nearly won over.

"But if we do pursue this avenue then there can be no turning back," he said in his sternest voice. "If the coin lands **HEADS** we call the chief of the constabulary immediately," he warned, pointing at the telephone beside his bed. "And if it lands **TAILS** then we pack this picture of yours in brown paper and you return to Scotland and never, ever speak of this matter again."

"Very good, Your Majesty."

"Big Ben? Big Ben?" the King called out to his loyal servant, who was waiting outside in the corridor.

"Yes, Sir?"

"Bring the sovereigns."

"Very good, Your Majesty."

A few moments later the King had the velvet pouch in his hand. Still he thought it advisable to take one extra measure.

"Big Ben, we are about to toss a coin on a matter of some significance and we wish you to bear witness. Without divulging the nature of the decision we seek, suffice it to say that should the coin land **HEADS** we make a telephone call; if it lands **TAILS** this trusted former employee of mine shall return to Scotland without another word being said."

"Very good, Your Highness."

The King spun the coin high in the air, which flashed gold in morning light, and which landed **TAILS**.

• • •

Later that morning it was arranged that the Sovereign would visit Malcolm Message in his nursing home.

By now in his eighties, Malcolm had stayed on at the palace for as long as he could after retirement age, but once he had broken his hip for the second time the King had arranged for him to be admitted to the private nursing home that he used for other employees who could no longer live independently. Of course Malcolm had missed his room at the top of the palace – where during daylight hours he could watch the King's subjects milling about the palace's gates; and then, once it was dark, trace the passage of aircraft as they passed silently through the night sky – but soon enough he had learnt to find peace in his ground-floor suite, which overlooked a garden of deep herbaceous borders and climbing roses.

No one had actually said Malcolm was dying, but it was clearly the case, the doctors having phoned the previous evening to say the King should come sooner rather than later if he wished to bid his faithful servant farewell. The King travelled in one of his disguises as he had learnt from previous experience how long these visits could take if he was recognized: everyone but everyone would want to shake his hand.

He found his subject asleep in his ground-floor suite. It was a warm August morning; warm enough for the doors to the garden to be open. Some birds, sparrows and blue tits, were feeding from a feeder, at times so thickly congregated they could have been bees hanging from a honeycomb.

"The King is here to visit you," a nurse whispered into the dying man's ear.

"The who?"

"The King."

At this Malcolm began to haul himself up in bed, like a boat over sand.

"Don't strain yourself, Mr. Message," the King tried

to stop him. "My visit can only be brief unfortunately. How are you?"

"Your Highness?" Malcolm gasped.

"Yes?"

"Your Highness, I wish to thank you."

"But it's me who should be thanking you."

Malcolm had opened his eyes by now, almost alarmingly wide. "I wish to thank you from the bottom of my heart. You see you saved me when I was at my lowest."

"And you have done invaluable work for us at the palace."

Malcolm looked at the Sovereign blankly.

"In both your capacities," the King explained. "Firstly as a plumber, carrying on the tradition of your noble family. The arrangements at the palace have never run so smoothly again since . . . Well, since those unfortunate days. But thankfully you were able to attend to our other, perhaps more pressing needs viz our *Health and Safety* arrangements. You have only to glance at the Accident Book today to see how much safer a place the palace is compared to how it was before you joined us from Norfolk."

"But Your Majesty . . . You don't understand: I wish to thank *you*!"

"And I'm saying it should be us thanking *you*."

Malcolm's frown was almost petulant. "Us? Who's us?"

"By us I mean the palace," the King replied.

"But Your Majesty . . . "

"Sit back a little Mr. Message."

"I wish to thank you personally, Sir."

The King thought it would be wise to accept this gratitude at face value. "Your thanks are much appreciated," he said.

As Malcolm sank back into the pillow, his cheeks hollow from the effort of breathing, the King reflected on the nature of these thanks. Whatever he did and wherever he went he was thanked. That was why he found sentiments of gratitude so hard to accept. In reality this poor man had lost his business (and his love) at the hands of Lord Embers, that private secretary of his of thirty plus years ago who had had his own ideas about running the household. How strange it was then that, three decades later, the King should still be dealing with the aftermath, he thought. Come to that, how strange it was that he had had occasion to speak to the present Lord Embers only the week before in connection with his illegitimate son from the capital of Argentina. And, of course, he had had a hand in this, too.

• • •

Thinking that he might not be returning to Scotland – that he might be detained by the police on account of the statement he imagined he would have to give viz. the drowning of Lord Embers – Nick Winter had only purchased a one-way ticket. At liberty to catch any train of his choosing then, he elected first to take a walk along the Thames.

Crossing the river on Vauxhall Bridge, he walked downstream, heading east. A little further on, close to Lambeth

Palace, he took a seat on a bench with a good view of the Houses of Parliament. It was high tide. Barges and pleasure boats passed one another, riding each other's wakes. Gulls hung above the river, like kites. Exhausted by the events of the morning, he fell into a deep sleep.

For the first time in years he dreamt of Freya. There she was sitting in front of her window, an abundance of green at her back. Naturally, Nick was nervous as to how she might receive him after all these years, but evidently time was of no consequence to her. That smile – simple, honest and filled with the warmth of an unconditional ally – was as fresh as it had been nearly half a century before. Not having enjoyed physical relations for some years now, Nick did not awake aroused - although a smile hovered on his lips as he remembered how Angela would whisper hoarsely into the pillow beside his ear:

"Not *another* hard Winter?"

It was just as he was considering this that a man sat next to him on the bench.

"Hey, don't I know you?" this person presently said in an American accent.

"I don't think so," Nick replied.

"Surely you recognize me?"

"I'm not sure I do," Nick insisted, rising to leave.

"It was a long time ago, admittedly, but look again. I'm Kai, the friend of Constancia. You took us both fishing on the Dee."

"Fishing?"

"You're the ghillie from Balmoral, aren't you? "

"I don't know what it is you're talking about. Good morning to you, sir."

And clutching the package containing Freya's portrait close to his chest, Nick took leave of the American to join the body of tourists and local office workers who thronged the thoroughfare.

• • •

"The darnedest thing," Kai told Cal later that evening. "You remember the story I shared with you about a boatman at Balmoral?"

"About a drowning, you mean?"

"Well, I sat down on a bench this morning. And there he was: the very same man!"

"You're certain?"

"Without a question of doubt it was him! But why deny knowing me, that's what I'd like to know? Why deny admitting who he was, even?"

The more the two spoke the more a sense of complicity grew around them, like an aura. The Californian and the London taxi driver had not seen each other for near on two score years. Yet within a matter of days here was one thing and then another: a series of incomprehensible coincidences. And all centred around Lord Embers.

"Do you think we should warn the King?" Kai asked Cal.

"I don't know, Kai."

"I mean perhaps the King would be interested to meet the person who drove the young man from Buenos Aires into the capital from Heathrow Airport? And once there we could bring up the subject of the ghillie. I even remember his name: Nick Winter. Yes, we must tell the King we've encountered Nick Winter. He may take the view it's all a coincidence. But you and I know all about coincidences. And so, too, does the King. Let *him* decide what to do with that information. I don't think it should rest with us. What have we done to deserve it?"

"I agree."

• • •

So they telephoned the palace and fixed up a meeting for the very next afternoon.

When the time came they were ushered into a morning room on the mezzanine level. The King had just been to the dentist and kept feeling his jaw where it was still frozen.

"Thank you for thinking of coming to see us with this information," he said once he had heard what the two men had to say, "but actually it's all in hand."

When both visitors looked perplexed, the King went on to explain:

"This young fellow whom your friend here collected from the airport . . . well, we interviewed him here at the palace only last week."

"You did?"

"And you were probably correct in thinking you saw Nick Winter yesterday morning. Was he carrying a parcel wrapped in brown paper by any chance?"

"Yes, I think he was."

"You see, he had come to collect a package from the palace."

"That being the case we are sorry to have taken your time, Your Majesty," Kai said, standing to leave.

The King waved them back down onto their seats.

"But naturally I am interested in the coincidental nature of these events, which do seem to be interconnected in some manner. How long did you say it was since you were last in London?" he asked the American.

"I've only ever been to London once, Sir, and that was when I came to visit you with Constancia in Scotland, all those years ago."

"It is rather extraordinary," the King couldn't help frowning, "when you think I hadn't seen Nick Winter for almost as long myself."

And seeing Kai frown, too, he went on with a careful explanation. He didn't mention anything about the trouble there had been with Nick Winter's wife; rather he stressed how natural it should be that, after the tragedy of the drowning of Lord Embers, the poor ghillie should wish to make a fresh start, taking up the post of boatman on a beat on a great salmon river in the Scottish Borders, a river with almost as many named pools as the Dee itself.

"But of Constancia, I have heard nothing," the King sighed. "I believe she now lives in New York. I've tried to keep in touch, which is the obligation of a godfather, but my impression is she would be rather left alone."

"I am sorry to hear that, Sir."

"Well, I can quite see that being the godchild of the King of England would not be to everyone's preference."

• • •

No sooner had Kai and Cal left the palace than the sad news came that Malcolm Message had passed away. The end, when it came, had been perfectly peaceful, thankfully. There had been no pain or distress.

"We must send flowers to Gwendoline Hargreaves, Big Ben," the King said. "Anemones, if you can find them."

"Yes, Sir."

"How strange life is!" he had occasion to comment for the second time in as many days. "The timing, I mean. How well I remember Edith and Gwendoline coming to the palace for the same job and the difficulties we had that day with that appointment. And then all the difficulties that followed with the plumbing contract, and the part Lord Embers played in it. And how now, today, we are still dealing with its fallout. I wonder if we aren't treading where we shouldn't, Big Ben?" the King mused.

"It is for His Majesty to decide these matters," the other replied.

"With privilege comes great responsibility."

Grace And Favour

Wishing to keep Mauricio out of trouble until he was at the airport and about to embark on the return leg of his journey to Argentina, the King had instructed that he and Bowen should stay in a grace and favour flat in Richmond. A chauffeur drove them there in a Bentley rarely used for official business on account of its colour, which was a dusky, mallard green. Having arrived where they were to be billeted, the two thieves walked laughing through its sumptuous rooms. They found champagne in a fridge and began to make merry.

"A million pounds! Congratulations, Bandito!"

"A million pounds is just a start," the other replied, gargling from a golden goblet.

"You mean you don't intend to leave on that airplane?"

"Not for one second."

"But how will you manage to stay? The King has many henchmen at his behest. You will be strapped into your seat like a chicken, whether you like it or not."

"I mean to make a great deal more than a million pounds," was the simple answer. "Then and then only will I return to my home country. And perhaps I will take you with me?"

"Why should I be interested in your barrios?"

"Because there you will find real heat," Mauricio

answered, sweeping his elfin-lover off her feet and carrying her, protesting wildly into the bedroom.

Just then there was a rap at the door. Like guilty children the thieves fell silent. Until, remembering their position, they began to laugh once more.

"And who are you?" Mauricio asked, opening the door to an old woman bent with age.

"You shall tell me who you are first, and why you are here before I answer that question," came the reply.

"My name is Mauricio and I am staying here on account of the fact that my father is Lord Embers."

"Lord Embers, you say?" the other questioned him.

"The very same. Now, who are you?"

"I was assistant housekeeper to the palace, and I have lived upstairs in retirement for the last quarter of a century. You have awoken me with your drunkenness."

"We are hardly drunk, Señora."

"Lord Embers, you say?" the old lady repeated.

"You don't believe me?"

"Certainly, I believe you."

"Then why keep pressing me?"

"I'll tell you why, because the Lord Embers I knew was a most disliked person."

And here the old lady embarked on a most informative discourse. In fact she had been one of the servants present in the palace's kitchen when the butler had related the very same facts to Malcolm Message in the presence of the then young Lord Embers. The old lady did not withhold a single detail. Indeed she seemed to relish the last part of the story.

"You mean my grandfather was murdered?" Mauricio demanded to be told.

"The water was high and the late Lord Embers was clumsy in the boat. Both of these facts cannot be contested. But he should never have perished. The ghillie was guilty of not saving a drowning man."

"And my grandfather's death has never been avenged?"

"As I say, the verdict was death by misadventure."

• • •

Mauricio was deeply troubled by these revelations. Once the old lady had taken her leave he returned to the bedroom in silence.

"These things happened in the past, Bandito," Bowen tried to reason with him. "What's done is done. You must put history to one side."

"This is not our code of conduct in the barrios, Bowen."

"What do you mean?"

"It is strange, is it not?" Mauricio mused. "I have no desire to make myself known to my father beyond, that is, glimpsing him in an airport concourse. But for my grandfather to have lost his life on account of the incompetence of a boatman: well, that is something else altogether."

"What do you propose to do?"

"I propose to put matters right, that's what I propose to do! This man shall come to see how we settle scores in Latin America."

"How will you find him, though?"

"I will find him, have no fear. Just as I will find the other person whose account is still open."

"And who might that be?"

"Why, the siren who abandoned me in Tierra del Fuego, that's who."

• • •

The following morning at 11 o'clock the green Bentley came to the grace and favour flat to take Mauricio and Bowen to the palace for the reception.

All day the young lovers had been enjoying each other in the bedroom, making free of the champagne on ice and feasting on titbits they had found in a second fridge. They had also found a vast array of clothing in the various cupboards, and after much merriment, dressing and cross-dressing, the two thieves had decided upon what they would each wear. Mauricio had chosen a pinstriped suit with wide lapels; Bowen a green dress that made her look like Maid Marion, if it wasn't for the cherry-red of her lipstick.

"Why are you driving so slowly?" Mauricio demanded of the chauffeur, as they made their way through the interminable maze of streets.

"I have instructions to have you at the palace no earlier than noon."

"Then I should like to visit a friend en route."

And Mauricio gave the chauffeur an address close to Marble Arch.

"This is where the siren lives?" Bowen asked her beau.

"She gave me an address, which I knew to be false. This one I found amongst her papers."

"And you are going to call on her now?"

"Not now."

"Then why are we going there?"

"We are going there because I wish to deliver a letter by hand."

• • •

The uniform that Lord Embers had used twenty years before when he had worked at the palace had been carefully stowed away, not least to protect it from the menace of moths, of which there seemed to be an abundance at the palace. It didn't take long for a seamstress to let it out to suit His Lordship's new figure.

"Why don't you stand there," the King told his godson, pointing to a doorway between two staterooms. "I shall engage the young man from the barrios in conversation, leading him from room to room on the pretext of introducing him to the assembled guests. He will, of course, be wondering who amongst the party you are; but have no fear: we have invited so many dignitaries that soon he will tire of his enquiries. Indeed, that is my aim: to present so many different possibilities that he will come to understand the random nature of selection."

"He will be attending with a young woman, you say?"

"Of not impeccable character, I'm afraid. This young woman, who goes by the name of Bowen, evidently took the young man from the barrios under 'her wing'. My investigators have informed me they have formed quite a close alliance."

This was the first time Lord Embers felt a pang. Not once had he wanted to know his illegitimate son over the past week, but now that another had a claim on the lad's affections he felt a lonely sense of emptiness and desolation. It bewildered him.

"Don't worry," the King reassured his godson, witnessing this passing cloud of ambivalence, "by this evening you and he will be at the airport and all this will be over."

"Quite so," the other agreed.

• • •

Twelve o'clock came and Lord Embers took up his position between the staterooms. Guests began to stream in; a band began to play. Great arrangements of flowers stood, like magnificent headdresses, on pedestals and filled the air with their delicious perfume.

Lord Embers was acutely aware that he must not actually catch his illegitimate son's eye: unable to account for his demeanour he may well have given the game away. It so happened that in the wardrobe room he had found a pair of round-framed spectacles, the lenses of which were just strong enough to distort his vision. By looking at his son through these, he thought, he would be able to maintain a suitable air of detachment and professional distance.

Presently there was a sense of the guests gently parting

to create space for the King; and seconds later he had his first, albeit blurred, glimpse of his son. Properly this time his heart went out. Mauricio had been torn from Constancia, roughly treated by Emilio, he must have weathered the most terrible privations in the barrios and where had he, Lord Embers, been to protect his flesh and blood? He had been designing buildings and altering the skyline, that's where he had been. Only suddenly these achievements meant nothing to him.

• • •

Mauricio, for his part, was carried away by the splendour of the staterooms and the finery on display. Particularly he was struck by the women, who wore every shade of pastel, the powdery colours enhanced by clasps of diamonds and other precious stones. This was exactly as the King had planned, and he led the young man from group to group, introducing him to some of the two hundred guests he had invited for the occasion.

"May I introduce you to Mauricio Jesus Gonzalez," he murmured to each they passed, quietly explaining to Mauricio who these people were.

"How do you do?" Mauricio said in his best English, bowing like a diplomat.

Not once did it really interest him who his father might be. Truth be known he would have liked any of these men to be his father, in so much as he did not know them and had no ambition to know them, either. Indeed he felt almost fortunate, seeing all these men gathered together in their finery, to have had no father at all. Yet he was determined to go along with the scheme.

"Everyone here is calling you 'Sir'. Is this how I should address you, too?" he asked the King.

"I find it easier than Your Majesty or Your Royal Highness," the other replied.

"And you mean to say one of these gentlemen is my father, Sir?"

"That is correct. We have organized things just as we agreed. There are two hundred and twenty eight guests here this evening, half of whom are women. Each man here, therefore, has a hundred and fourteenth chance of being your father."

"One hundred and fourteen to one?"

"In betting parlance, quite so, yes."

"And later this afternoon, before I board my flight, how will I know my father?"

"We shall go through the departure lounge together in our disguises. Your father will be waiting there. He will be wearing a white Panama hat."

Panama hats were common in Buenos Aires, both downtown and in the barrios.

"There may be any number of people wearing Panama hats," Mauricio objected.

"This hat will have a ruby-red hatband."

"I see. And when will I see the money, Sir?"

"You can see it now, if you wish?"

"Yes, I think I do rather wish."

So the King led Mauricio through an antechamber and into a small room beyond, a sort of inner sanctum. Milo, one of the Prendice brothers, was standing to attention, clearly on guard. Behind him, on a cushion of red velvet, lay an attaché case. The King snapped open its catches.

"I know we settled on a million," he said to Mauricio, "but you will find a million and a half in here. You see, I appreciate how painlessly we have come to terms."

"Thank you, Sir."

"And may I ask what arrangements you have for Bowen?"

"Bowen, Sir?"

"We have a seat on the aircraft reserved for her, too. If you had plans to take her to Argentina, that is?" the King enquired.

Mauricio had no real attachment to Bowen and for this reason had not properly considered this question.

"Yes, she will be coming with me," he answered anyway. "And may I thank you for your foresight in this matter."

"The pleasure is mine. Well now, having concluded the business here at Buckingham Palace, I think it is time we set off for the airport. We must change into our disguises first. Milo, meet us outside with the attaché case in thirty minutes."

"Very good, Your Highness."

The King took Mauricio into still another inner sanctum. Presently Bowen joined them. She was flushed from her success at the party. One of the King's equerries had chaperoned her through the throng: the gentle manners of all assembled and the compliments she had received had been something new altogether.

"I saw your father," she whispered to Mauricio as two

seamstresses wheeled in racks of clothing from which the three were to choose their new attires.

"And which one was he?" the other nonchalantly asked.

"He was dressed as a footman."

"A footman? My father? Impossible!"

"You didn't see him looking at you through his spectacles? Perhaps you need spectacles yourself."

"*Spectacles*? Are you sure?"

"Perfectly."

"So tell me: this man who you have identified as my father," Mauricio then asked, with not quite the same nonchalance, "he was tall? Or short?"

"Neither."

"But of my build?"

"How could I tell? He just seemed like an ordinary footman."

• • •

Things were not going to plan with Lord Embers, however.

For an hour he had stood stock still between the staterooms, not batting an eyelid as his illegitimate son followed the King from one room to the other and then back again. But all the while he had been observing him. It seemed in only sixty minutes he knew everything about his son, even the way he would smell if he were to embrace him.

"Big Ben, I can't go through with this," he cried as he contemplated his own rack of clothing.

"It will all be over in a short while, Lord Embers," the other tried to encourage him.

"I can't . . . I simply can't . . . "

"Would it help to articulate your feelings, sir?"

"The boy is my flesh and blood. For twenty-one years I have done him the most terrible disservice. I can't just let him go like that . . . see him board an aircraft and then no more. I know what we have arranged makes rational sense, but I'm sorry, I simply can't go along with the King's plan."

"What will you do, sir?"

Lord Embers was almost hysterical. "I don't know," he cried all the harder. "I mean, you met the boy, didn't you, Big Ben? What did he say? Did he actually say he didn't wish to meet me?"

"He said exactly the same as you, sir. That he would like to 'behold' you."

"Behold me?"

"His English doesn't allow him to express himself quite so succinctly, but that is the impression I had, sir."

"Oh Big Ben, how I wish this had never happened!"

• • •

And so when Mauricio, Bowen, the King and the Prendice brothers arrived at Heathrow Airport's departure lounge, Lord Embers was nowhere to be seen.

"There must be some delay, we must be patient," the King kept repeating.

"Possibly he's in another disguise?" Mauricio cheekily suggested.

But when another half an hour had passed and still

there was no sign of Lord Embers, Mauricio took a firmer line.

"Well, this is all very well and good, but I wonder how this charade appears to you, Sir?" he began. "In good faith I paraded myself amongst two hundred and twenty eight guests at the palace, not to mention the scores of staff who were there in attendance, too," he added with the faintest tilt of the head, "and now that it is my turn to see my father – my flesh and blood, no less, the man who came to South America to sow his seed and then return to his burrow, like a rabbit . . . Why, he is nowhere to be seen!"

"It *is* very awkward," the King had to concede.

"Awkward? I see it as being more than awkward. In fact I consider it to be a breach of contract. And being as such, there are two facts that have made themselves crystal clear to me."

"And what are they?'

"The first is I shall not be boarding the aircraft as proposed. How could I weather the sense of anticlimax this whole procedure has engendered? The second concerns the matter of the million and a half pounds, which I now consider to be mine outright."

"My dear fellow!"

"You don't agree? Well, consider it this way. If I had wagered on an outcome of an event with you and lost, do you really mean to say you wouldn't protest if I didn't settle up?"

"We didn't take a wager, though," the King objected.

"We entered into a contract, which is in essence a wager.

And as the contract has been broken I do not think it right that I should forfeit the stake we had agreed upon. Do you think I have gone between one disguise and another for nothing?"

"Why not take half the money?" the King suggested.

"It's all or nothing, Your Majesty," Mauricio replied. "If Mr. Prendice here doesn't hand over the attaché case I shall have no hesitation in throwing off my disguise and explaining my situation to any journalist who might see fit to make enquiries."

"That's blackmail!"

"Call it what you will, but these are my terms."

Knowing that Mauricio and Bowen would not be able to go far in the Kingdom without being under surveillance, the King waved his consent to Milo, this man handing over the money.

They were indeed under surveillance, and not only by Ernest Prendice, who had been observing developments from one of the many food outlets in the airport's departure lounge, but also by PJ and his men. This group had been waiting at the gate, hoping for a chance to steal whatever it was Mauricio and Bowen had in their possession before they boarded the plane.

And so it was that when the two lovers began to make their journey back into central London by taxi, they were being followed by two sets of spies.

• • •

At first the King was furious with Lord Embers.

"What do you mean by not keeping to our arrangement?" he demanded on his return to the palace.

Lord Embers was still dressed as a footman. "I'm so sorry, Sir," he cried.

"I've lost a million and a half pounds. Not that the money's important – only it is rather a lot. Well, hadn't you better explain yourself? And how you intend to proceed?"

"I'm so sorry, Sir," Lord Embers repeated his apology. "I was simply incapacitated by the most overwhelming sense of yearning and longing. I know I have no right to these feelings, yet there they were. And as far as knowing how to proceed: I am afraid I am at a complete loss," he finished, almost swallowing his own words.

Seeing his godson in such distress, the King took a more sympathetic line.

"Of course I can see your position *is* very awkward," he sighed, throwing aside his disguise, the headwear of which had left a scar-like impression across his already troubled brow. "I mean supposing the young man from the barrios *did* welcome some form of relationship with you: what could or would you do? Set him up here in London? In some sort of profession? Or make visits to Buenos Aires? You see, it's much more of a problem than it appears."

"But he didn't say he wished to know me, did he, Sir?" Lord Embers tremulously asked.

"I can only be honest in reporting that he expressed no such wish," the King was quick to reply.

"Then there is the answer to my woes! I shall just have to live in silence with the consequences of my actions."

"Lord Embers, you must not feel sorry for yourself! There are many much worse off than you! Promise me that you will never forget that!"

"I will not, Sir."

Just at that moment, the Prendice brothers were ushered into the room. They looked flustered and their clothing was in a noticeable state of disarray.

"Well?" the King invited them to explain. "What news? Where are they?"

"I very much regret to say we lost them, Your Majesty," the older of the brothers replied.

"Lost them? How so?"

"We followed them to a street in Uxbridge, where their mini cab took a turning down a cul-de-sac. Thinking it wise not to follow but to wait on the main road, it was some time before we went on foot to make our enquiries."

"And?"

"They had made off down an alleyway, Sir."

"And you didn't follow them?'

"The alleyway led to Goldhawk Road. I'm afraid they clean gave us the slip."

The King was fed up with apologies. "So where on earth are they?" he cried, throwing his hands in the air.

"We did make enquiries with the mini cab driver."

"And what did he say?"

"He said he overheard his fares making plans to go to Scotland."

"To *Scotland*?"

"That's what he said, Sir."

• • •

Once the King had dismissed the Prendice Brothers and Lord Embers had taken his leave, too, he called out to Big Ben.

"Big Ben, Big Ben?"

"Yes, Your Highness?"

"Have them prepare the royal train. We leave for Scotland first thing in the morning."

"For Scotland, Sir?"

"A drama will unfold there, I have no doubt, and we must be on hand to intervene."

"You're quite sure, Sir?"

"Quite sure."

• • •

The Prendice brothers may have lost Mauricio and Bowen, but not PJ and his accomplices. The cul-de-sac down which the two thieves had apparently vanished was well known amongst petty criminals – and cabbies, too, for that matter – as a convenient getaway. Indeed it was known in the underworld as "The Looking Glass".

It only remained for PJ and a single accomplice – for he had dispensed of the others by now – to await their appearance on the Goldhawk Road, like gamekeepers waiting for rabbits to be flushed from their warren by ferrets. Then, maintaining a safe distance, they tailed the black cab the young thieves had subsequently hailed, shadowing it across London to Kings Cross Station. And from there followed them onto the next departing train for Scotland.

• • •

Desiring to speak to Mauricio alone on account of the potential complexity of the matters he wished to discuss with him, PJ had to wait until they were past Darlington before making his approach.

"Well, blow me down! If life isn't full of strange coincidences!" he exclaimed with feigned incredulity, sliding into the vacant window seat opposite Mauricio's. "If it isn't our friend from the Rio Plata!"

"Do I know you?" the other gruffly answered.

"Why, you came to see me in *The Osprey* just three days ago, unless I'm very much mistaken? There was a matter of some," and here PJ lifted a finger to the corner of his mouth, "a matter of some gold sovereigns."

"You have followed us here. What do you want?"

"Only to be of assistance."

"What can you know of my business?"

"Perhaps more than you think."

Mauricio gave his most sickly smile. "In which case you'd better speak up, only I warn you: my patience is limited."

"Patience is indeed a most precious commodity, and I can see I shall have to put my cards on the table," the other said, leaning in a second time. "Unless I am very much mistaken you are the son of Lord Embers."

Being an experienced card player himself, Mauricio was able to keep a perfectly straight face.

"The son of Lord Embers? Are you serious?" he laughed. "Nonetheless I would be interested to learn how you have arrived at this theory."

And so PJ began to explain. He had only said that life was full of strange coincidences, because some fifteen or twenty years previously, when he was no more than a runner in *The Osprey*, he had found himself held overnight in a police cell in Marylebone. With him was a young man clearly of a different class and standing, and very distraught at his predicament besides. In common with extremity of circumstances, the tongue had loosened; and through the course of the night this young man had explained his position pretty much in full, producing a gold sovereign concealed on his person to provide substance to his story.

"When you came to see me at *The Osprey* last week," PJ went on, all the while pretending to gaze at the scenery that slipped past and so giving the young man from the barrios the opportunity to scrutinize him as closely as he desired, "when you came to the inn and spilt these sovereigns on the table between us . . . well, I knew at once their provenance."

"That doesn't explain anything about my identity. Anyone could have stolen those sovereigns."

"Indeed. Only there is the stamp."

Mauricio was unfamiliar with this term. "The stamp?" he repeated.

"I spent the course of a whole night with Lord Embers," PJ explained, "from sun down 'til cock crow. We were in a cell no larger than a bathroom. His features I came to know well, they are not the kind of features you tend to forget . . . and I see them replicated before me now."

Mauricio, who had not had the benefit of seeing his father at the airport, did not know if he resembled his father or not.

"I don't believe a word of this," he said, "and my patience is now at an end."

"Only perhaps it was the peculiar nature of his story

that made his features so indelibly unforgettable," PJ went on, raising his hand in a holding gesture. "And when I say peculiar, I mean singular."

"Go on."

"You see, it seemed this young Lord had lost his father in an accident on a river. Only there was some question as to the nature of that accident – whether it was by misadventure or not. Of course, how could he – or anyone else, for that matter – know? There being no witnesses, you understand. And in any case what happens in these simple accidents of fate tends to happen with such deftness," PJ finished with a shrug.

Mauricio sat forward and fixed PJ with a steely look. "You had better tell me what you know."

"I would imagine things are rather the same in Argentina as they are here," the other replied, indicating the attaché case that Mauricio had tight under his arm.

"Rewards are always generous," Mauricio replied, "otherwise they would go by a different name."

"That's well put, if I may say so."

"You'd better not waste any more of my time. Now speak up!"

"Very well. Allow me to begin with a statement. You are heading to Balmoral with this young lady, are you not?" PJ stated, gesturing at the empty seat.

And when Mauricio did not answer, he went on.

"You are going to Balmoral because you wish to see where your grandfather perished. And having surveyed the scene, for whatever good it will do you, you then wish to interview the man who was with him that ill-fated day.

How do I know this? I know it because this was exactly the same journey the present Lord Embers was embarked upon as he described it to me that night in the cells."

"Then what stopped him?" the young man from the barrios demanded, rising in his seat.

"Why, the King stopped him! That's who stopped him."

"The King?"

"Our Sovereign believes in manners, he doesn't have recourse to passion."

"You'd better go on."

"So, for a consideration we have yet to agree, I can furnish you with details – not about the river, which you will find flowing the same course as it wends its way through forest and gorse – but about the man who was there that day. His name. And the town in which he now lives and works. For he no longer resides at Balmoral, I can tell you that now."

"You seem to know a great deal about this subject."

"Only from what I can remember."

"After so many years? Your claim on a reward is growing thinner by the second."

"I have a peculiar capacity for recalling facts. *The Osprey* is my preferred public house, but there are many others I have frequented over the years. I tend to remember facts by their names. There are two public houses in Bermondsey that hold the answer to your question. One is called *Boswell and Johnson*; the other goes by the name of *Jack Frost*."

• • •

On leaving the palace, Lord Embers had not gone straight home. Instead he had spent some time alone to collect his thoughts in the bar of a Knightsbridge hotel. When eventually he reached his house, it was to find his wife fast asleep in their bed. Exhausted by the day's proceedings, he crawled in beside her and was soon asleep himself . . . only to have the most terrifying dream.

He dreamt he was in the East End of London at one of the sites he was developing there, a brand-new hotel in the Modernist style. In fact this hotel was so modern it was to have an outdoor swimming pool on its roof. He was standing there with his partner, Christian, when suddenly they became aware of the heat of the setting sun.

"Isn't that a strong sun?" Christian commented.

"It is rather," Lord Embers heard himself agreeing.

They thought about it no more and went on with their business. There was a problem with the height of the balustrading: obviously this must conform to building regulations, but perhaps it should be glass in places, Christian was suggesting, so that bathers could actually see over the capital from their loungers. Lord Embers found himself having difficulty in concentrating, as once again the strength of the sun seemed a little unusual.

Then, suddenly, Christian said: "**LOOK!**"

Thereafter the most terrible chain of events began to unfold. The sun, instead of sinking into a setting position, they could see now was actually rising, so slowly at first you couldn't be sure. Then there was no doubt about it: the sun was inching upwards through the afternoon sky.

In fact it was like a comet, dragging a tail, a fireball of the most indescribable intensity, in its wake. Not only that, as it was gaining height and speed, it seemed to be breaking up, with satellites being shed in every direction, each careering off in its own blinding heat ball of fire.

It was obvious that this was the end of the world. In the dream Lord Embers blamed himself for being so unprepared, for not having anticipated this now obvious potential calamity. Of course the sun, the one element upon which life depended, might disappear! Then his attention focused itself on the streets. As yet there did not appear to be any material alteration to the normal course of life, but soon lights would start going out. The world at large would know its destiny. Perhaps in only a few hours the whole of civilization would be lost.

And what was the last thing – or the first thing – Lord Embers needed to do? It was to see his son in order to say goodbye to him. And not the son who was sleeping safely in the next-door room, beneath a quilt of tropical fish and crabs . . . but this prodigal son of his who was at present en route to Scotland.

VI

In Scotland

It wasn't difficult to track down Nick Winter. There was only one salmon river of repute in the Borders, Kai discovered, and a directory of beats to lease for angling – along with the contact details of the boatmen who worked on those beats – was freely available to any who sought it.

But when he reached the Gardener's Cottage, a simple house in the Scottish style of timbered eaves and white-washed render, he did not find Nick at home. Rather it was his wife who came to the door. Trusting by nature she may have been, but strangers were seldom seen in these parts, especially one so casually dressed in dusty trousers and a corduroy shirt.

"My husband is away from home," she told the Californian. "It is fishing you are after?"

"Not fishing."

"Then what else can have brought you here?"

"If truth be told I'm not sure," the American had to confusedly admit.

"And what kind of an answer do you call that, pray?" the ghillie's wife retorted, pulling herself up.

"Mrs. Winter, has your husband ever mentioned an accident that befell a certain member of the Royal

Household?" Kai asked. "A private secretary by the name of Lord Embers?"

"And his account of it could not have been clearer," the other returned. "My husband was ghillie then on the beats of the Dee at Balmoral when Lord Embers, in losing his balance in the boat, subsequently lost his life. I wonder how your visit here today could warrant the arduous journey you have evidently undertaken in order to reach us? The details of the inquest being so well documented, you understand?"

"The fact is I have come to seek a resolution of sorts," Kai said by way of answer.

"A resolution of what sort?"

"You see, I was staying at Balmoral just a few weeks after the tragedy, having travelled there with a godchild of the King's," the American explained. "Your husband took me fishing on the Dee, on the very same stretch on which Lord Embers had lost his life. I had a very strong sense of the tragedy then, no doubt owing in part to your husband's distress at the events. But the fact is," Kai went on with more purpose, "what happened on the Dee has had an impact on my life, too. It would be wrong to say that it was akin to harbouring a secret, but somehow this drowning was to become like a dropped stitch in a tapestry. My eye kept returning to the imperfection. A fanciful metaphor, I know, but somehow the accident in which he was involved, it was to become an impediment or obstruction beyond which I could not pass."

Mrs. Winter had taken a step over the threshold in order to close the door behind her.

"You come unannounced to this simple house to worry a wound," she said to the visitor. "You speak of tapestries, dropped stitches, impediments and obstructions. I would ask you to turn about and retrace your steps from wherever it is you have come."

"Mrs. Winter, will you at least tell your husband I have called on him this morning?" Kai broke in.

"And who shall I say it *was* who called?"

"Just tell him it was the man who, the day before yesterday, was seated beside him on a London bench."

At this Mrs. Winter regarded the visitor with more interest.

"If what you say is true and you were sat on a bench with my husband in London just two days ago, then you will have seen that he was carrying an item?" she said.

"Yes, he was," Kai confirmed, "he was carrying a package, a package wrapped in brown paper. He had just been to collect it from the palace."

"Well, you can take it," the ghillie's wife told him, stooping to produce the same from inside the porch.

"I take it?"

"Its true significance I may not fully comprehend: all I know is that it has no place here."

And with this she closed the door on Kai, who had no option but to turn his back on this simple abode with its heavy eaves and whitewashed render.

• • •

Meanwhile Mauricio and Bowen had just reached St Boswells themselves, where it had taken their taxi just one pass up the simple high street to locate the town's only sporting shop. Soon they were inside this store, where a fresh-faced girl was standing in front of a cabinet of shotguns and rifles, an incongruous sight to say the least.

"And what if my friend here, a visitor from overseas, wished to take an afternoon's angling?" Bowen asked the girl with the glowing cheeks. "To whom should we apply?"

"It depends on where you would like to angle," she returned, reasonably enough. "On a private beat or on club water?"

"Oh, on a private beat, of course!"

"And would your friend be in need of a ghillie?" the girl then asked.

"Indeed he would. In fact we have an idea we know who we are looking for. If the name Jack Frost means anything to you?"

"Now I don't think it does, but if you wait here just a moment I will make enquiries of my father."

This man, the proprietor of the tackle shop, was soon standing before Mauricio and Bowen. He had been tying salmon flies in the back room and came carrying a reel of tinsel in one hand and a cape of hackles in the other.

"Thank you for the courtesy of your enquiry, but I am sorry to disappoint: there's not a ghillie in these parts who goes by the name of Jack Frost. None that I know of, anyhow."

"When we say we have an *idea* the man's name is Jack

Frost," Bowen interrupted the other, "we use the word in its most literal sense. You see," she explained with a coy smile, "we have come to Scotland on the back of a riddle."

"On the back of a riddle?" the owner of the tackle shop repeated, clearly amused.

"A mischievous fellow it was who guided us here. By means of wordplay – on the names of taverns, no less! Our first clue was a public house in Bermondsey, which he told us was called *Boswell and Johnson* – that is why you see us before you in St Boswells. The other public house went by the name of *Jack Frost*."

The girl with the glowing cheeks was smiling to herself: evidently she found this explanation and the appearance of Mauricio and Bowen an engaging novelty, too. Then suddenly she had it!

"You mean Nick Winter, don't you?" she interjected.

"That's exactly who we mean!" Mauricio applauded her.

"Nick Winter, of course!" the father seconded his daughter, striking the counter with a glancing blow, which made the spools of gut shake on their spigots. "Just tell us when you'd like to go fishing and we can organize everything from here."

• • •

Also recently arrived in St Boswells was Lord Embers. Having taken the first available flight to Edinburgh from the City of London Airport, he had almost beaten his son to it, and was well ahead of the King, who was still some two hours away, his train having stopped briefly at York.

Before leaving the capital, he had instructed his secretary to make a reservation for him at *The Weir Pool* – the best hotel the town could offer – and soon he was eating a plate of scones in its simple dining room. The meal concluded, he took the lift up to his bedroom, where, exhausted by nerves and worry, he pulled the curtains shut and lay down to take a nap. Sleep would not come to him, however, in spite of the mattress being soft and the sheets lightly perfumed. Most likely this was on account of the nightmare he had suffered a few hours since. Indeed, the more he revisited that rooftop scene with its half-constructed swimming pool, the more restless he became.

But this was nothing compared to what happened next. Rising from his bed to throw back the curtains, he stood for some seconds staring blindly out of the window, wondering if he hadn't been seamlessly transported from one dream sequence into another. For there, below him on the high street, accompanied by a young woman in a country coat . . . and now making their way into the hotel's *foyer* . . . was his son.

Pulling himself away from the window, Lord Embers paced from one end of his hotel bedroom to the other. This was the reason he had travelled north: to meet the man to whom he had given life. But what was he going to do? Take the lift back down to the reception area of sporting trophies to make some form of introduction? Hardly. Like a thief who has been surprised by the unexpected return of a householder mid-burglary, he opened his door an inch or two to better appraise the situation. There were footsteps on the staircase, the sound of the proprietor . . . and then the sound of his own son's voice.

"We do not wish to be at the back," came an unfamiliar accent, thick and plain-speaking. "Why be above the kitchen when we can be above the street."

"Those at the front are our premium rooms," the proprietor politely explained.

"By that you mean what?"

"By that I mean they command a higher rate."

"I'm sorry we didn't make ourselves better understood. We require the best rooms the establishment can offer."

And so Mauricio and Bowen were shown into the room next to Lord Embers.

A second time, like a caged animal, Lord Embers measured his room. For twenty years he and his son had lived an ocean apart, an unknown quantity to one another. Now they were in adjacent hotel rooms! How could this possibly have come about? His instinct told him to check out of *The Weir Pool* without delay, return to London on the next available flight, never to think of his son again – yet he couldn't. Taking a glass from beside his bed, he entered the bathroom and moved its rim, like a stethoscope, over the wall above the bath. Until at last he found a place where he could hear the young lovers speaking in the next-door room.

"Bandito, you must take care where you put that case."

"How so?"

"Someone will try to steal it from you."

"You refer to that knave on the train?"

"Have it signed for in the hotel's safe."

"Do you think I look crazy?"

There then followed what can only be described as a romp. There was something viscerally exciting about overhearing others making love, but this didn't pertain when it was one's own flesh and blood, Lord Embers discovered. Soon, thankfully, the activity was at an end, and a second time he listened by means of the glass on that area of wall above the bath.

"And what do you propose to do when you find this boatman?"

"I mean to gauge his reaction when I remind him of his carelessness."

"And then wreak revenge?"

"Possibly."

"You will find yourself in prison."

"I have been in prison before and do not mean to find myself there again," came the dull response.

At this Lord Embers recoiled from his position between the bath and the sink, almost dropping the glass as he did so. His son had been in *prison*? It couldn't be true! But if it was, what could it mean? That Mauricio Jesus Gonzalez was no more than a common criminal? A thug? A thief? Or worse, perhaps? Never before had Emilio's warning of the curse of his estancia rung so loudly in Lord Embers' ears.

• • •

Normally when they were travelling by the royal train, the King would direct that their headquarters should be set up in a discreet siding. But this time, owing to the fine weather and the wildness of the country, he had decided that they would billet at a remote inn.

His first orders on their arrival there were to instruct the Prendice brothers to find Nick Winter and bring him to this place without delay. Thinking he would wait in the tranquillity of the garden, a table was prepared beneath an alder. But no sooner had he sat in the shade of this tree than he was on his feet again, pacing up and down the course of a small stream (known as a burn in Scotland).

"Where is he? Where is he, Big Ben?" he kept muttering under his breath. "You know I find waiting intolerable."

"I'm sure he'll be with us imminently, Sir."

"I have been an agent in creating the situation in which we now find ourselves," he kept repeating, like a mantra. "Where did I go wrong?"

"If I may say so, Sir, you were only doing your best," the other replied.

"But what if my best wasn't my best?"

"It was difficult to know how to proceed, Sir."

"You're quite right: one forgets that. It was indeed impossible to know how to proceed."

Finally the news came that Ernest Prendice's car had reached the inn. Only it wasn't Nick Winter who approached the King over the rough lawn of tussocks – it was the Californian, Kai Nelson.

"It's you again!" the King cried.

And once Ernest Prendice had taken leave of the two, having briefly described the manner of his encounter with Kai in the vicinity of the ghillie's cottage, the King turned on the American:

"So you didn't actually see Nick Winter, then?"

"Only his wife," Kai told him.

"But why had you gone there? Why are you here in Scotland at all?" the King wanted to know.

"I felt compelled to come," was the answer.

And when the King pressed him further Kai repeated pretty much word for word the explanation he had given Mrs. Winter just a few hours since.

"I'm not surprised you were shown the door!" the King snorted. "And I'm not sure I don't concur with your own analysis, too, since I find what you say very fanciful. What can you mean by dropped stitches and obstacles?"

"It's a gut feeling, Your Majesty."

"My dear fellow, you can't go through life acting on hunches! I mean, are you telling me you are some kind of psychic?"

Kai could have been just as dismissive of the King's sovereigns. Yet, out of politeness, he limited himself to replying only: "Of course not!"

"Then what?"

"No one can know for certain what happened that afternoon on the Dee, no one being there to bear testimony," Kai answered. "But it's my intuition that there is more to the accident than was reported, and I have come to Scotland today because it seemed only the right thing to do. If I had not encountered Nick Winter in London last week then perhaps I would not have given the subject too much further thought," he frowned, "but to find myself sitting next to this man on a bench . . . after forty something years . . . admiring another of your fine rivers . . . well, that was too much of an invitation to act. Indeed, to decline would have been akin to swimming against the current."

"A most unfortunate use of metaphor, if you don't mind my saying," the King broke in imperiously. "But if I may ask," he then demanded, indicating the package Kai was holding under his arm. "What is that?"

"Mrs. Winter gave it to me," the American answered, handing the parcel over to him.

"Mrs. Winter gave *this* to you?" the King repeated, roughly tearing one corner of the brown paper enough to reveal, as he feared, the Pre-Raphaelite picture. "Why?"

"She simply said it had no place in her house," Kai went as far in answering.

The King took a deep breath. "I must say this is very strange, very strange indeed," he whispered, almost lost for words.

"What's strange, Sir?"

"Well, when you came to see me with your friend, the taxi driver, in Buckingham Palace last week and I asked you whether my ghillie, the man next to whom you sat on a bench in Vauxhall, was carrying a brown paper parcel, well, this is the same package."

"And Mrs. Winter gave it to me? Why?"

"That I cannot answer."

"But what is its significance?" the American pressed the Sovereign.

"I fear if I tell you it will only excite your quizzical nature, Mr. Nelson. But the fact is that when Nick Winter came to see me at Buckingham Palace last week, he came to speak of this very picture," the King said, withdrawing it properly from its wrapping.

"He did? Why?"

"He came with a story of how, in his mind, it had played some part in the tragedy that unfolded on my beats of the Dee."

And the King went on, not catching the American's eye, to briefly outline his exchange with the ghillie of a few days before. How apparently Lord Embers' instruction to remove the painting from the wall outside the rod room at Balmoral had engendered such a sense of resentment that it had gone so far as to precipitate the accident that had occurred on the river later that morning.

"So there *was* an argument?" Kai said, sitting back.

"We cannot know that for sure, Mr. Nelson.'

"He's admitted as much, though."

"Yes . . . but knowing the character of the man as I do, having spent so much time alone in his company, I find it simply *impossible* to believe," the King said with emphasis. "My conviction is that the man became deranged by the tragedy, and remains so, the passage of the years only making the condition more pronounced. Doubtless the poor fellow suffered terribly as a result of the accident that befell Lord Embers. I mean how would you or I have felt if a man had drowned before our very eyes and we had been unable to save him? A terrible weight of regret and guilt, I imagine," the King answered the question. "Indeed perhaps it was this remorse you 'picked up' on when you came to visit me at Balmoral all those years ago?"

"Of course that's possible," Kai had to admit, "it's an established fact that sentiments of regret and guilt, whether justified or not, do have the capacity to attach themselves to a host, like a parasite. But if I may be so bold as to ask: Why are you here, Your Majesty?" the American then had the temerity to enquire.

"I am here out of a sense of responsibility," the King replied. "Not only am I involved in the affairs of Nick Winter in so far as a ghastly tragedy was played out on my river, but I am also intimately involved in the affairs of another person who, as it so happens, also has a connection with this tragedy."

"You refer to the man from South America?" Kai chanced.

"I do. And perhaps it would interest you to know more about this man?" the King suggested with a careful look.

"Naturally I would be interested to know more."

"The man from South America has an English-born father, Lord Embers, as you know already. But his mother is from Argentina."

And here the King revealed the identity of this woman: Constancia Acosta, his favourite godchild.

"No!" Kai gasped.

"So, you see, things are a little more complicated than even someone with a sixth sense might imagine," the King ruefully stated. "Doubtless the complexity appeals to your sensitive nature," he went on with more tact, "as it is indeed a coincidence that you should find yourself sitting next to my ghillie after forty something years. And a coincidence, too, that this man from the barrios should be the son of the woman with whom you were on such intimate terms at the time of your visit to Balmoral."

"It's incredible," the American kept shaking his head.

"And having a somewhat superstitious nature myself, perhaps I do consider that you may be part of a grander scheme of things, its purpose we are at present unable to establish. But I would ask you to put aside these superstitions, and if you were able to do that, then perhaps you could be of assistance?"

"I would be intrigued to know how?"

"We can only surmise why this man should be in the Borders and it doesn't bode well," the King said with a gesture to the moving water beside them. "But I am determined that no tragedy should arise out of his presence here. If you were able to put all considerations about the ghillie to one side and instead help to create and promote a sense of benevolence and harmony, then I think by so doing you would be pursuing a good outcome instead of worrying the past, picking at a scab, which I am convinced is misguided in any case."

"I think I would be prepared to assist," Kai replied

after a moment of careful thought, "but only on one condition."

"What condition?" the Sovereign haughtily asked.

"That you desist from betting."

"You refer to the coins?"

"Your Highness, with respect: you must stop gambling!"

• • •

To book his day's angling and to hire all the tackle and equipment he would require – waterproofs, rods, reels and salmon flies – Mauricio had used the name Maurice Bowen.

At the appointed hour, then, laden with this tackle and wearing a pair of thigh waders, he made his way down a path of hairpin bends to reach the river. There he found Nick Winter waiting for him by a simple fishing hut of lapped timber. Having introduced themselves by way of exchanging the briefest of pleasantries, they were soon afloat, the sound of broken water gently tap-tapping beneath the bows.

"And is this a dangerous river when it's in spate?" Mauricio asked once they were some way over.

"It can be," the other replied, addressing the boat's wake (for he was rowing with his back to Mauricio).

"You've had casualties here, then?"

"By that you mean what?"

"By that I mean it is possible to drown here?"

"I would say it is," came the simple answer.

They were by now a distance of about forty metres

from the far bank, travelling crab-wise across the river to compensate for the weight of its current.

"It might interest you to know that a relative of mine lost his life on a river similar to this," Mauricio went on. "My grandfather, no less. The tragedy occurred long before I was born – indeed I believe my father was barely born himself – but, of course, time is of little consequence in matters of life and death. What's done is done in these simple accidents of fate, wouldn't you agree?"

"I wouldn't like to say," Nick Winter muttered, tightening his grip on the oars.

"A simple accident of fate, it was said," Mauricio went on, breezily, "only the circumstances surrounding the tragedy were never entirely satisfactory. It wasn't in question that the gentleman was a clumsy fellow. In the excitement of playing a fish, you see, he found himself pitched overboard. But what was never properly established was whether, once in the water, the ghillie made sufficient efforts to save him."

At this Nick Winter turned in his seat. "I wouldn't call that man a gentleman," he scowled.

"So you didn't try to save him?"

"Of course I did!"

"Then perhaps you would like to tell me exactly what did happen?"

"I will not!" the ghillie said, filling his chest. "For the simple reason that I have nothing further to add to the statement I made at the inquest, a transcript of which is available to any who care to read it."

And with this he turned his back on Mauricio and began to pull at the oars once more.

"Inquests!" the man from the barrios cried, incensed. "All I hear is talk of inquests! Well, perhaps it's time for me to make an inquest of my own."

And with this he stood, and placing his right foot behind the starboard rowlock, brought his whole weight to bear on that side of the boat. In a flash they were both in the water. At first, trapped beneath the capsized hull, the ghillie was nowhere to be seen; then he was free, clawing at the air, like a drowning pup. As quick as a weasel Mauricio was on his back, pressing down on his shoulders, submerging his head and neck beneath the peaty water.

In this fashion the two men were washed downstream, through one gate of white water and into the next, until finally they had arrived at an island of loose stone. Here the man from the barrios hauled his victim onto the shingle with his strong forearms of bronze.

"My friend, if you value your life, you had better tell me what happened."

"I will! I will!" the ghillie cried.

And so here, beneath the canopy of beech that overhung the Tweed, Nick Winter made peace with himself, his god and another human being. His confession to the King in London had been lacking through omission: no stone was left unturned now, no detail overlooked.

"Believe me when I tell you, Mr. Bowen, I myself don't know what happened exactly," he explained. "I was frustrated by Lord Embers' treatment of me – he had lost his fish and he was angry – but that was no excuse, of course it wasn't. There was general confusion in the boat . . . and for a fateful moment I saw red."

"You mean to say it was a crime of passion?" the man from the barrios put to the ghillie.

"Exactly that. A moment of disregarding consequences . . . of being content to act in the moment only. But believe me, sir, I never intended for Lord Embers to perish. Not for one second. My life was a misery from that day forward, from that moment forward. If only I had been able to save him. But he was held fast by a branch and the current was too much for him."

"In effect you did murder my grandfather, then?" Mauricio asked the confessor to confirm.

"I did," the other admitted, "I did. It was an accident, but an accident that was initiated by a purposeful act and I must take full responsibility for the end result. In the same way that those accessible to a crime must be held accountable for it in spite of their innocence of the deed itself."

"Stand up, my friend," Mauricio told the ghillie, releasing his hold of his victim's lapel.

And once the two men were standing and looking squarely at each other in the eye, he said:

"You can promise me on your life that you would have saved my grandfather if you had been able to? That he would have lived, and perhaps he would be alive today, if he hadn't become impeded by this obstruction you refer to?"

"On the lives of my grandchildren I can promise you that," the ghillie swore. "It is a sight that has been branded on to me, one that I have never been able to banish – even in my sleep. To stand there and see Lord Embers caught by the ankle, his head trailing beneath the water, to stand there and to know that through an impulsive act of mine a man had lost his life, it is something I have never been able to come to terms with."

"Then you have suffered enough," the man from the barrios pronounced.

"I have?"

"And it only remains for me to thank you."

"You to thank *me*?" the ghillie sobbed.

"For your honesty. Certainly you are guilty of a crime. You tipped a man – my grandfather, no less – into the water, where he was to meet his end. But chance has played a part in this tragedy, too. And in this world chance is one element over which we have no control."

"There is truth in what you say," the ghillie was now restored enough to concede. "But why thank me?"

"If you had lied to me – and believe me, I have a nose for lies – who knows the outcome of our simple fishing expedition," Mauricio smiled.

"Oh god," Nick moaned.

"But do you know, I feel some sympathy for you," Mauricio said. "Besides, it would interest me to hear more about my grandfather. You say that he was a rough man, yet still I would like to have an impression of him. And also the court in which he worked, by which principally

I mean his employer, the King. Come now, let's sit here awhile, the water at our feet, and talk some more."

• • •

All afternoon Lord Embers had been in his room. He had watched his son leave the hotel alone; thereafter he had listened to the movements of the young woman in the wax coat by means of the tumbler against the bathroom wall. For ages, it seemed, she was on the telephone, sometimes speaking in a whisper, at other times with more animation. Finally he thought he could hear her preparing to leave her room, and then the door clicking in the way it does when the departing person wishes to keep their business private.

He was right: a few moments later he saw the girl in the Barbour jacket, this time with her hair tied in a ponytail, step into the street below. In her left hand she was carrying an attaché case. If this was the same case that had been the subject of the conversation Lord Embers had overheard by means of his improvised stethoscope, then this girl was making off with it, like a thief. Lord Embers swept his jacket from behind the door: he would not stand by and watch this young woman make off with his son's property.

He was soon outside. The simple high street being busy with people heading for home after work, it was not difficult to follow Bowen without her knowledge, so determinedly did she walk and so tightly did she clasp the briefcase in her left hand. She took a right turn by the post office, and then entering a car park made her way directly to a navy blue car in which two men were clearly waiting.

Lord Embers had to run the last twenty yards to prevent the car driving off, getting there just in time to push Bowen aside and to slam the back door that was being held open for her. With his other hand he grabbed the attaché case. This occasioned an immediate response from the driver of the car and his passenger, who seeing the object of their interest about to slip through their fingers, threw open their own doors and, spilling into the car park, bore down on Lord Embers.

It was rather like the time the young Lord had fought off the robbers in Green Park to keep possession of the sapphire bracelet the King had commissioned for Constancia. Or the time he had fought in the garden of his childhood home to take possession of the gold sovereign the Californian had brought south from his visit to Balmoral all those summers ago. In fact as he wrestled with his adversaries both contests were vivid in his mind. And perhaps gave him additional strength, for before long the urchins from London could see they were fighting a losing battle. Moreover the *fracas*, like a catfight, was attracting the attention of the general public, some of whom were now close by and clearly about to offer their assistance. The upshot was that the two men, with a screeching of tyres, which left the air acrid with an unnatural aroma, were able to drive off un-apprehended. With or without Bowen, it was unclear.

Lord Embers was left panting, fighting for breath. But what was important was that he had prevailed: the attaché case was safe in his right hand.

"Are you okay?" a member of the public asked him.

"Perfectly, thank you."

"Hadn't you better be looked over by a doctor?"

"Believe me, they suffered more than I did," Lord Embers assured the knot of well-wishers, surprised by his choice of words, since they could almost have been spoken by his own son.

Taking refuge in a public house close by, he ordered himself a dinner of roast chicken and potatoes. He had no wish to return to his hotel, where his son may or may not have returned to take up residence in the bedroom next to his own. What he needed was time to work out where he stood in all of this, to know exactly what he was going to do next.

There was a good fire in the small chamber annexed to the dining room, and, having eaten, he took one of the wing-back chairs from in front of the fireplace and moved it a fraction so that he might stay out of view of the *foyer*. There, with the attaché case jammed between the small of his back and the armrest, he fell asleep.

• • •

The King and Kai had continued to sit at that table beneath the alder, where the Sovereign said they should wait for further intelligence from the St Boswells area (this time from Milo Prendice, who had stayed behind when Ernest had brought the American to the inn).

Lunch was eventually served, which consisted of soup and a roll followed by herring in breadcrumbs. It was so refreshing to eat outside at the foot of the heather-clad hills, the plaintive cry of moorland birds carried on a fresh afternoon breeze, that both men quenched their thirsts by each drinking two pints of bitter shandy.

The King was naturally interested to know more about Kai, especially with regard to his gambling.

"I don't believe there is a cure for this condition, only a reprieve," the American explained. "I may not have taken a wager myself in twenty years, but that's not to say I haven't relinquished my belief in the workings of chance, in spite of everything," he stated.

And when the King asked him to clarify what he meant, Kai described his experiences at the hands of his father-in-law in Reno. How this man, a casino owner, had recognized the indelible mark of the gambler, and had made his own plans to cure it.

"He insisted I came to work for him."

"For the House, you mean?"

"Day upon day I sat in a windowless office," Kai frowned, "surrounded by a sea of monitors. 'No one can win against the odds, it's impossible,' my father-in-law would say to me at the start of every shift. 'Don't get up until I tell you – find me the cheats'."

"So you were cured?"

"Cured perhaps, but a lesser man as a result, I fear."

"And what do you mean by that?" the King nervously asked.

"I mean only that there is romance in the notion of luck, is there not? That you can find yourself in that place of perfect stillness, aligned with, if you will pardon the expression, a power greater than oneself."

"Yes," the King murmured, clearly moved.

"That like peering through a keyhole suddenly you are looking through a second keyhole beyond – which grants you access to that realm where, in spite of the casino's margin, you can sit down at the tables, hold yourself in that swim for long enough to walk out of the doors a rich man."

"What's wrong with being a romantic?" the King tried to make light.

"Because perhaps my father-in-law is right: that perhaps ultimately life cannot be navigated on whim alone."

"Even when it is impossible to know how to proceed?"

"Even then. We must always be seen to take responsibility for our actions."

"By whom?" the King laughed.

"That is the question!" the Californian laughed, too.

Just then Ernest Prendice approached over the lawn. "We have two pieces of intelligence, Your Highness," he announced.

"And?"

"The first is that Lord Embers is in St Boswells."

"Lord *Embers* is in St Boswells?" the King repeated. "You mean to say my godson?"

"He's staying at *The Weir Pool*, Sir."

"Foolish boy! He'll wreck everything," the King said with unrestrained force. "Can't he ever stick to his initial purpose? And the second piece of news?"

"It's regarding Nick Winter, Sir."

And here Ernest described how his brother had shadowed the man from the barrios down to the banks of the Tweed, where, from a position of concealment, he had watched on as this man had set off in the boat with the ghillie. How, subsequently, midstream, the two men had fought in the water. And then how they had sat on an island of loose stone for some forty minutes or more. On what appeared to be amicable terms, even shaking hands when parting company.

"They shook hands?"

"That's what I've been told, Sir."

"But how extraordinary! What were they discussing?"

"My brother was seated close by in the undergrowth, close enough to intervene should matters have gone the other way, but not close enough, evidently, to hear even one word of their conversation."

"You say they parted on friendly terms, though?"

"That is what I have been informed."

"Mr. Nelson, there is the answer at least to one of our troubles!" the King declared, exhaling one great breath. "That is indeed an enormous relief! Whatever it was that was discussed it looks like trouble has been averted. Thank heavens for that! But how very strange. I must go to St Boswells forthwith," he said, rising with the Pre-Raphaelite picture held tight to his chest.

"Wouldn't it be better to wait, Sir?" Kai countered, rising, too. "To let the dust settle, I mean."

"No, no. I must make myself available to my godson: he may need my guidance. After that I must visit my faithful ghillie – to satisfy myself that all is as well with him as has been reported to us here. It is my duty, no less. And you, good sir," he finished with an upraised finger, "you must remain here. Remember our arrangement. It may well be that you can assist further in matters should they require any further resolution."

• • •

It was dark when Lord Embers eventually emerged from the pub to make his way cautiously back up the high street. The curtains were drawn in the bedroom next to his own, he could see: so in all likelihood his son and his son's lover would be in occupation. He stopped at Reception and spoke to the young girl on duty there, arranging to have the attaché case placed in the hotel's safe. Then he climbed the stairs, rather than taking the lift, to his floor.

This time when he placed the glass against the bathroom wall it wasn't a romp he heard: it was the bullying tones of his son.

"Tell me again what happened," was the repeated demand.

"I've told you a hundred times," came the tearful reply.

"Twice you've told me, and twice you've contradicted

yourself. That is why I want a proper account of what happened."

"I told you. I was going down to ask for shampoo, and when I came out of the lift two men, accomplices of the man with one earlobe, were coming towards me."

"I don't believe a word of it. How could they possibly have known we had a room here? Unless you told them, of course."

"Check yourself if there isn't shampoo."

"I'll teach you to speak of shampoo."

And here Mauricio must have tightened his grip, as his lover gave a pathetic whimper.

"Bandito, you're hurting me . . ."

"If there is one thing I will not tolerate it is deceit and lies."

What could Lord Embers do? In the next-door room a man from the barrios – his son no less, the person he wished to be reconciled with more than any other – was abusing a young woman. God only knew what torture awaited her at the hands of this uncouth man. He should pick up the phone and call the police at once. There was really no other option available to him. With a trembling hand he lifted the receiver. It was the same girl who had placed the attaché case in the hotel's safe who answered.

His voice a thick whisper: "This is Lord Embers in Room 28."

"Yes, Lord Embers?"

"Put me through to the police."

"Certainly, sir. But Lord Embers?"

"Yes?"

"There is someone in Reception who would like to see you."

"Who?"

"The King."

• • •

It was indeed the King. He was wearing a tweed jacket and matching plus fours with rust-coloured stockings, these of such good quality they could have been the ones he was wearing the afternoon old Lord Embers lost his life on the Dee. Big Ben was dressed in a similar fashion, only his stockings were of gunmetal blue.

"Robert, come and sit down," the King said, half rising from where he was seated beneath a trophy salmon encased in convex glass. "How are you?"

"A little at sea," Lord Embers admitted. "You see my son is upstairs. In the room next to my own."

The King gave a wince of sympathy. "I know. May I ask . . . have you, how can I put it, introduced yourself to him?"

"No," Lord Embers shook his head, "I've been rather at a loss, you see . . ."

And here he summarized all that had passed in the last few hours. How his son had taken up residence in the room next to his very own; how the young woman with the ponytail had attempted to steal an attaché case which was evidently not hers; how, in a car park, he had fought with two ruffians; and how he had heard his son offering this young woman violence, believing her a traitor, or at any rate someone he could no longer trust.

"Of course *I know* she's untrustworthy, having witnessed her treachery first hand," he finished. "But what's in the attaché case, that's what I'd like to know?"

The King had taken off his deerstalker and was fiddling with a lure that was embedded in the tweed. So much confusion was in evidence, it was imperative that there should be transparency now.

"Robert," he began, "there is something I must tell you."

"Yes?"

"In London we arranged it so that you might see your son at a function at Buckingham Palace and then, afterwards, your son might see you at Heathrow Airport before boarding an aircraft. In both instances neither was to know the identity of the other."

"And?"

"The fact is, Robert, your sentiments were perfectly straightforward and honourable. You simply wished to behold your 'stamp', for want of a better word. But I'm afraid your son, Mauricio, had travelled overseas with a different motive. He had come to the UK to gain, in a manner of speaking."

Lord Embers was quick to see where this was headed, perhaps on account of the King's expression, which was almost too sickly sweet to countenance.

"You mean you paid him off?" he whispered.

"Robert: that attaché case you fought over: it contains a million and a half pounds."

Lord Embers sat back, his mind a cauldron of confusion. "So really he has no interest in me at all?" he cried. "He has just come to the UK to be paid off, is that it?"

"That's not quite how I would have put it."

"Oh god!"

"Robert, not so loud."

"And then why is he here in Scotland? How does he even know about the tragedy that befell my father on the Dee?"

"A retired employee of the palace informed him, I believe," the King answered.

"And you mean to tell me he's come all this way to wreak some kind of revenge?" Lord Embers whispered. "On my behalf?"

Here the King thought it wise to quickly intervene. "In fact they have already met," he said.

"They have? And what transpired?"

"There was an incident, an altercation of sorts," the King frankly admitted, "but it would appear, thank heavens, that everyone is safe."

And here the King repeated all that he and Kai had learnt from Ernest Prendice: how Milo had shadowed Mauricio down to the Tweed, and from a concealed position, witnessed their fight in the water.

"They fought in the water?"

"And then fell to talking. Of course my detective couldn't overhear their conversation from where he was hiding, but from their demeanour it would seem they parted on good terms. Indeed the two men shook hands after their discussions."

Lord Embers frowned, disbelievingly. "Perhaps *I* ought to meet this ghillie?" he said, forcing a bitter laugh. "Perhaps I'd end up shaking his hand?"

"That I cannot answer, Robert."

"So where does all this leave me?" the distraught Lord despaired.

"It leaves us with the question of your good self. You have seen your son as we agreed in London at the reception I organized, but it seems you were unable to proceed to the airport, where he was to 'see' you. Perhaps you don't wish him to see you?"

"But I do! But I do!"

• • •

At that very moment there was a commotion in the reception area, a slamming of doors and raised voices.

"Bandito! Don't go!"

"Get out of my way."

"Be reasonable."

"You ask me to be reasonable when all that surrounds me is duplicity? Prepare my account," Mauricio was then heard to be ordering the girl at the desk.

By now the King, Lord Embers and Big Ben were standing in the doorway of the lounge in which they had been holding their meeting. They could see Bowen pulling at her lover, beseeching him.

"Where are you going?" she wailed.

"Back," he growled.

"Back where?"

"It was a mistake to have come angling here when the real fish are in London," he spat, throwing his haversack over his shoulder and pushing her properly aside.

To reach the street Mauricio had to pass within feet of the three men who were still standing, like spectators, in the lounge's doorway. As the King and Big Ben were in disguise and not yet having had the benefit of seeing his birth father, the three men were, to all intents and purposes, strangers to him. Yet he seemed to pause a moment. As if on account of the valet's height perhaps he did recognize Big Ben, after all. For this reason he looked more carefully at the King. And then more carefully still – albeit without a shred of recognition – into the eyes of Lord Embers.

Then he was gone.

"Where is he going, Big Ben?" the King was heard to ask.

"Back, Sir."

"You mean back to Argentina?"

"No, Sir, I rather think he means back to London."

"Then we must follow post-haste – in spite of the fact we've only just arrived. Come on, Lord Embers, wake up man!"

"One minute, please," the other said, raising his hand and heading to the desk.

The attaché case was soon retrieved from the hotel's safe. Only once it was fully open did Lord Embers dare to look down. To find it empty.

VII

In London

Around this same moment in time, after a long day on the *Eurostar*, Arabella was returning to her flat in London's Maida Vale. It had been an extraordinary weekend away. Her boyfriend, Angus Weatherall, had proposed marriage to her beneath the Eiffel Tower. And she had accepted!

So joyous was the sense of occasion that they were soon making love again. This time on Arabella's sofa, their naked bodies impeded by the kilim cushions of coarse weave, yet seemingly only more determined to make union in spite of them. When it was over Arabella began to open her mail. Drawn to the first envelope on account of its unfamiliar handwriting, she read:

"*Siren, many thanks for the dollars and for extending my stay in* El Crillon. *I feel I owe you.*"

"Oh god!" she whispered.

"What is it?" her fiancé asked.

"Nothing."

"Nothing?"

"Last year I met someone on my travels in Chile. I don't remember giving them my address, that's all."

"Them?"

"Him."

"A lover, then?" Angus laughed.

"No, a travelling companion."

"And now he's in town?"

"It would appear so."

Angus, still laughing, tried to feed his hand between Arabella's thighs, which she involuntarily tightened.

"What's the matter?" he asked her now.

"I just wasn't expecting to hear from him, that's all."

"Nothing to worry about, though?"

"Nothing at all. Only I don't remember giving him my address. It's not something I would have done. In fact I *didn't* give him my address," she was sure, making her way to the bathroom.

• • •

Soon enough they were in bed, and soon enough Arabella began to dream.

She dreamt she had taken a coat to the dry cleaners, where they had told her it would need a special treatment. Foolishly – for Arabella was not a wealthy woman – she had failed to obtain an estimate of what this treatment would cost. When she returned to collect the coat there were, in fact, two coats waiting for her. Each with a bill in an elaborate envelope: one red, one yellow. Opening the first she saw, to her horror, a figure of £570 owing. When she asked how a coat could possibly cost so much to clean, the young girl who was on duty could offer no explanation. The second envelope was opened. A bill for the same amount! Whatever was she to do? She needed one of the coats – it was cold now – but could in no way afford to pay £1,140.

Here Arabella awoke to find a man seated at the end of her bed. At first she thought it must be her fiancé; then sensing Angus's sleeping form beside her, she thought she must still be in a dream. Not for long, though.

"Hey!" she shouted, the blood ice in her veins.

"Quiet!" the man told her.

"Angus! Angus!" she then cried.

"What?" her fiancé grunted.

"There is a man! Wake up. Do something!"

Soon Angus was sitting up beside his fiancé, blinking madly, swallowing hard. "What the fuck!" he exclaimed.

"Now you listen to me very carefully," the intruder began, addressing Angus first. "I'm going to say this once and once only. You have exactly sixty seconds to get dressed. And then a further thirty to let yourself out into the street."

"Okay, okay . . . "

"Keep listening. That postbox at the end of the square . . . you know the one I mean? Go to it and wait there. When I've finished in here," he said with a menacing look at Arabella, "I shall come to let you know you are free to go."

"Yes, okay . . . "

"But don't worry, I shall be watching you. One false move and this person here, to whom I have something to say, will suffer."

And here the intruder, who appeared to have a malformed ear, lifted a finger to his throat.

As soon as Angus had left the flat, this man instructed Arabella to place all the jewellery she possessed in a heap on the sitting room table. Not being a wealthy woman the most expensive item she owned was the engagement ring that Angus had placed on her finger the previous afternoon.

"That's everything?" the intruder pressed her.

"I have very little," Arabella answered.

"Now it is your turn to listen carefully. You will not report this incident to the police, do you hear? If you do things will not look so good for you. You understand that?"

"I do."

"Consider yourself to have been treated lightly."

And with this PJ left the flat.

• • •

The first person Arabella called was her friend, Maud Menzies. Living as she did under a flight path in Richmond, Maud had to listen very carefully to what she was being told.

"You poor *thing*!" she gushed once Arabella had finished recounting her terrifying story.

"It was awful, Maud, just *dreadful*. He was the most frightening man I've ever seen, he had part of his ear missing."

"But he didn't touch you?"

"He was sitting on my bed!"

"You poor darling! You're quite sure about the Argentine connection?"

"It was the way he said 'consider yourself treated lightly'."

"Anyone could have said that, though."

"Coming so close on a letter that says 'I feel I owe you'?"

"And what about Angus?"

"Oh, that's over," Arabella said, as throwaway as she could.

"Arabella!"

"How could I be the mother of children to a man like that? A man who goes to wait in the street, like a puppy. In a way I'm glad this has happened now and not later," she tried to put a slant on it. "I need a lion . . . not a mouse."

Once she had rung off, Arabella burst into tears. In truth the matter was more complicated than she had made out. Angus was the eldest son of a marquis, and would one day be the steward of many thousands of acres. In Paris he had told her of the life that awaited them. There were extensive mineral rights on both of the estates the family owned, he had confided in her. Quite simply they would want for nothing.

Arabella hadn't smoked for years, but now she found the *Marlboro* packet a friend had left behind on a visit one afternoon.

"Damn," she said, blowing a plume of smoke onto her knees.

• • •

Later that morning Cal was filling his taxi with diesel when he took a call from Kai.

"I need your help," the Californian wasted no time in coming to the point.

And as briefly as he could he described his trip to Scotland: how he had tried to see Nick Winter but how, instead, he had seen the King.

"I am here in Buckingham Palace right now as his guest. I came down with him last night on the royal train. There is going to be some kind of play-off in this Embers business – it's plain as day – and I have told the King you should be here, too."

"But why?" the cabbie quite reasonably asked.

"Because I need your support, Cal."

"I'm not so sure, Kai," the cabbie demurred.

"If you change your mind you know where I am."

• • •

Cal went about his work, taking one fare and then another. But it was hopeless. And so strange. For forty years he had sat in meetings of *Gamblers Anonymous*, listening knowingly as others described their battles with obsession, never for one moment imagining it would be necessary for him to fight that battle again. Yet here he was, passing Buckingham Palace only a few hours later, as if with another pair of hands on the steering wheel.

Big Ben came so quickly to the gatehouse of the King's Pictures, he may as well have been waiting there for him.

"Follow me," he said.

This time they ascended by a back staircase, where every inch of wall space was taken by pictures, some very ornately framed, and where light from chandeliers of cut crystal spilt a glittering glow. Yet Cal could not help noticing how frayed the stair carpet was and how there was the unmistakable evidence of mice and moths. Finally they reached the nursery, a room filled with glass cabinets containing every conceivable type of stuffed bird.

"Cal, I'm so relieved you've come," Kai said, jumping up from where he had been lying on the chaise the King used to meditate amongst his lifeless specimens.

"So many dead birds, Kai," was all the cabbie could say.

"They are the King's passion."

After they had embraced – which is the way in *Gamblers Anonymous* – they stood before a window that overlooked the quadrangle of terracotta asphalt.

"Now, my friend, tell me what all this is about? And how you think I can help?" Cal asked his friend.

As succinctly as he could, the American related all that had passed in Scotland: his visit to the ghillie, the purpose not to confront Nick Winter, but in some way to make himself known to him; how he had been intercepted by a detective and taken to where the King had set up his headquarters in the environs of a lonely inn; how, there, the Monarch had described the significance of the picture that now stood on an easel next to the fireplace.

"This picture?" Cal asked, scrutinizing it carefully.

"It seems the ghillie had an attachment to this image. Not only in his waking life but in his sleeping one, too."

"By which you mean what?"

"By which I mean he used to dream of this woman."

"And because he believed the King's private secretary had had it removed he caused the boat to capsize? I'm sorry, but don't you find all this a little far-fetched?"

"I don't know what to think," Kai frowned.

"In any event it was the King himself who had had the picture removed, wasn't it? Did he give any reason why?"

"He said it was the words '**UNTIL WE MEET AGAIN**' that had resonated with him."

"'**UNTIL WE MEET AGAIN**'," Cal repeated the phrase with an amused frown.

"He explained to me on the train last night how those simple words appealed to him – perhaps on account of the fact that they promised a time when, at the conclusion of his duties, his responsibilities would be at an end."

"You mean they spoke of a freedom of sorts?"

"Exactly that."

"Well, that's all very well and good," the cabbie went on, more serious now, "but whoever had this picture removed from its position outside the rod room door in Balmoral Castle, and why ever – don't you feel you have invested enough energy, a lifetime's energy, no less, in this particular story of yours? That as a guest of the King over forty years ago you were given a hex of sorts?"

"Not so much a hex – more a stain, perhaps."

"But why have you allowed this stain to subsist, to prey on you as a superstition?" the cabbie asked, studying his friend more closely still. "You don't believe this painting is responsible for your ill-fortune, do you? For the death of your wife, the destruction of your property by fire?"

"No, I don't."

"Then what?"

"All I know is that a lifetime has passed and soon I shall be buried next to my wife – but in that time the mystery of what happened on the Dee . . . it has somehow managed to cast a shadow over my destiny."

"My friend, doesn't our programme remind us to keep only our side of the street clean? Not to expend too much energy on the business of others?"

"What you say is true, of course. And yet there is something about this image," Kai insisted, returning to the picture, "which *is* deeply familiar."

"It's no more than a figure in front of a window, Kai," Cal was equally persistent.

"You're sure?"

"Absolutely sure."

And when his friend would not respond, Cal asked:

"Where is the King, anyway?"

"He is at a funeral."

• • •

Malcolm had wished to be buried next to Edith, to which Gwendoline had given her consent. So a simple affair had been arranged, again at Gunnersbury. Knowing there wouldn't be a crowd, the King had not bothered with a disguise.

After the service, the mourners made their way to *The*

Ampthill Arms. There was the same light drizzle, and once again, in time-honoured tradition, a fire burnt in the hearth. The King sat next to Gwendoline, where she was perched on the fender.

"I am so glad relations remained cordial between you to the end," he said to her. "It is to be commended."

"They were more than cordial," the other replied. "And largely thanks to you, Sir."

The King didn't feel he deserved any thanks. "But I only succeeded in making his situation more difficult," he replied.

"You refer to the plumbing business?"

"If only I'd been more aware of 'matters' in my household, the company may well be still thriving today."

"Your Highness, you must believe me when I tell you that Malcolm came to see that the end of that business was a blessing, for him anyway."

"But he was so depressed when the company went into liquidation. I mean, didn't you go as far as travelling to Switzerland?"

"He was depressed initially, granted. But that job you gave him at the palace: it was the making of him."

"He had only such a small room on the top floor, though."

"It was all he needed. Not having inherited his grandfather's ambition to make money, his expectations were correspondingly modest, too. He told me it was the management of men he found so tiresome."

"I find it tiresome, too," the King sighed.

"He was only interested in assessing and managing risk."

"Well, he certainly excelled at that!"

On the way back to Buckingham Palace the King reflected on what Gwendoline had said. That, in effect, good had come out of bad. In which case, perhaps what had happened all those years ago with the plumbing business and the previous Lord Embers hadn't been so bad after all, he considered. Not that it could be said that the tragedy on the Dee had had any kind of a silver lining, he was only too quick to remind himself.

Indeed it was this that most preoccupied the King as he waited in queuing traffic. It hadn't been a complete surprise to find the ghillie's manner so measured and distant when he had gone to call on him after leaving *The Weir Pool*. What had been most upsetting was to be told how a full confession made at the time of the tragedy would have been preferable to the years spent living in the twilight of semi-concealment.

The King felt understandably contrite about this, as it had been he who had tried to lessen the burden of guilt by making reference to the bet he had made with his private secretary at the start of that fateful day's fishing; but he hadn't expected his ghillie to confess all this to the man from the barrios. Least of all had he anticipated that there would be mention of the sovereigns.

"I do not wish to inculpate you with your talk of wagers and simple accidents of fate," the ghillie had said, "but if I'm honest, Sir, your sovereigns did me no favours. Ultimately, of course, it was my decision as to whether or not I held my peace, but all I know now is that I feel a great sense of release for having confessed in full."

"By 'in full' I hope you don't mean everything, Nick?"

"Everything, Sir."

"Even about the sovereigns?"

"Even the sovereigns."

At this the King had risen from his seat. "But don't you see you shouldn't have mentioned that?"

"Why not?"

"Our arrangement was that on the direction of the coin you were never to speak of the matter again. Don't you see it's rather bad luck to challenge an edict of that nature?"

"Bad luck for whom, Sir?"

"Well, for everyone," was all the King had been able to answer.

When it was clear that the ghillie was unwilling to volunteer anything further on the subject by way of an apology or otherwise, the King had then tried to return the Pre-Raphaelite picture.

"I take it you will have no use for this, then," he said, indicating the package he was now proffering in both hands.

"Sir, I no longer require it," had been the simple answer.

• • •

It was past noon before Mauricio reached London. He had planned to travel back to the capital by sleeper – which would have been a novelty for him – but had been unable to obtain a berth. So he had spent the night in a hotel close to Edinburgh's Waverley Station.

"I rather liked the accommodation there, a little dusty but bright enough," he told PJ, who had come to meet the morning train. "It was called *The Caledonian.* I think I should rather like to stay somewhere like that here in London," he said, lifting a hand to the traffic that streamed past them on the Marylebone Road.

"I know just the place," PJ assured his South American comrade, "it's called *The Ritz.*"

• • •

Soon enough the two men were alone in a top-floor suite of this hotel. *The Caledonian* must indeed have been dusty, as the first thing Mauricio did was to test all surfaces with a lazy wipe of a finger. Satisfied, he joined PJ at the window, which being south-facing afforded a view of Buckingham Palace.

"You think the King's in there right now? In his palace?" Mauricio laughed.

"Can't you see the flag?"

The man from the barrios knew nothing of flags.

"You mean he waves a flag when he's in residence? My friend, this man shall come to know the truth before long."

"You must proceed with stealth and care," PJ warned the other. "You have limited knowledge of how things work here. It is a good thing indeed you have made my acquaintance. Which brings me to the matter of our arrangement."

"The present time is never too soon to honour

commitments," Mauricio nodded, reaching for his haversack. "Only perhaps, to keep everything above board, first you might show me the fruits of your own endeavours?"

"Certainly."

And here PJ produced the engagement ring that just a few hours since had been on the fourth finger of Arabella's left hand.

"A ring of such splendour!" Mauricio whispered.

"An engagement ring," PJ explained.

"She was to be married, then?"

"There was a man asleep beside her."

"And this man: he fought with you? For his honour and for that of his betrothed?"

"He went like a lamb."

"Tell me what he said, I must know," Mauricio shouted with laughter.

"'Okay, okay', I think were the words he used."

"*Ay, Dios mío!*"

"And what of the girl in the wax coat?" PJ asked by way of returning to the subject in hand.

"It was exactly as you said," was the nonchalant reply.

PJ made a cursory show of searching for the attaché case. "She made off with your property, then?"

"I regret to say she did."

"But you prevailed?"

"If I hadn't I wouldn't be in a position to furnish you with this," the man from the barrios said, handing the other a *Caledonian Hotel* envelope.

For a moment it seemed PJ might have at least broken

the envelope's seal to check the colour of the notes within – he didn't, however.

"So what to do now?" he asked instead. "Your business is concluded?"

"Far from it."

"By that you mean what?"

"By that I mean I need to meet with the King in order to make some final arrangements."

"And how will you do that?"

"How will I do that? Quite simple: I shall telephone him."

• • •

Lord Embers did not head for the office on reaching London. He made straight for the palace. Because his flight had been delayed on account of fog, it wasn't until late afternoon when he finally appeared.

"I want you to meet two visitors," the King told him outside the Green Room. "They are here to help us."

"Who are they?" Lord Embers asked.

"A Californian and his friend, a taxi driver."

The journey had been arduous and Lord Embers couldn't help expressing exasperation. "How can they help?"

"One of them, the Californian, was at Balmoral shortly after your father's demise on the River Dee. His friend, the taxi driver, is an expert on gambling."

"On gambling?" Lord Embers repeated.

"The situation we find ourselves in came about as the

result of an ill-judged wager, and I will be the first to acknowledge that I have not improved matters by seeking clarification from the sovereigns I keep for difficult matters. The Californian has a place here as he was implicated in our difficulties from the outset. It was he who suggested that the taxi driver, a sort of sponsor in the world of *Gamblers Anonymous*, be in attendance, too."

"*Gamblers Anonymous*?" Lord Embers repeated, aghast. "But where is my son?"

"I do not believe we shall have to wait long to have that question answered. But first you must meet the visitors."

And taking Lord Embers by the arm, the King led him up the back stairs to the nursery, where they found Cal and Kai seated in two armchairs beneath a tableau of stuffed humming birds. The King was careful to introduce Kai in the vaguest terms, thinking it the most tactful way.

Kai was equally tactful, too. "Forty years passes more quickly than one cares to consider at this time of life," he said, shaking Lord Embers' hand, "but forty years ago it was that I encountered a beautiful woman, a woman more beautiful than I had ever seen before. We met in the Amazon, in a place of such dense jungle we were warned not to leave the path, as to do so one might become lost and so spend an eternity of time in searching for one's point of entry. It is my understanding that you found this woman, whose name was Constancia, irresistible, too."

Lord Embers could have been embarrassed, instead he was curious. "You mean you were on those type of terms as well?"

"We were," the American answered. "We were young

and carefree. On our return from Balmoral we parted at the airport, Constancia to visit friends in Europe, myself to return to my home in California. It was the type of relationship whose significance only becomes apparent at a later time, if you know what I mean?"

"And what are you doing here?" Lord Embers asked, turning to Cal.

"I am a taxi driver," this man answered, "and it was I who drove your son into the capital last week."

"And how did you find him?" Lord Embers asked with a diffident smile.

"I can only say I found him a perfect gentleman," Cal did not hesitate in replying.

Just then word came that there was an urgent telephone call for the King. The Sovereign didn't like to be disturbed when he was in the nursery and for this reason no handset was kept there. The call, therefore, had to be taken in the passageway outside.

"Yes, tell them I shall come now," Kai, Cal and Lord Embers heard the King confirm. "Yes, now."

And a moment later he repeated the same intention to the three men assembled.

"The man from the barrios is in residence in *The Ritz*, and I am going there to meet with him now."

"One thing, Your Highness," Kai said, stepping forward.

"Yes?" the King impatiently answered.

"You remember our arrangement? There's to be no gambling."

• • •

Considering it best not to be overly punctual, and thinking, too, that it might be an idea to take some air – a great deal had already passed so far that morning, after all – the King decided that he and Big Ben should walk across Green Park to *The Ritz*. Their disguises – suits of crushed cream linen and Palm Beach sun hats – couldn't have been wholly convincing, as more than the occasional walker they passed stopped to gaze at them with expressions of vague, oneiric recognition.

They were given no trouble at the hotel's desk, however, and were soon waiting to gain entry outside Mauricio's suite.

"It's you!" Big Ben exclaimed as PJ opened the door to them.

"Do come in, won't you?" this man invited them over the threshold with a vulgar flourish.

The suite had a third room beyond the sitting room, a conference room of pale, jasmine yellow. Here Mauricio was waiting, at the head of a glass-topped table.

"Gentlemen," he said, with a bow of the head to each.

"Good morning to you, sir," the King said, removing his hat.

Some small talk followed, the King enquiring about Scotland with Mauricio agreeing that it was indeed uncommonly beautiful, almost as beautiful as those parts of Argentina it so closely resembled.

"I even had a chance to cast a line," he finished.

"And did you do any good?"

"Nothing to hand, sadly. All in all, though, it was a most interesting visit."

"I'm so glad to hear it."

"But we must come to the point," Mauricio said, indicating that all parties should sit.

"Indeed," the King agreed.

"I'll be plain with you," the man from the barrios began. "Much as I have enjoyed my visit to your Kingdom, I do now wish to return to my home country, there being some business to attend to there, you understand. Only I find there remain some matters to resolve here, too."

"Oh yes?"

"The first being that once more I find myself impecunious."

"And the second?"

"There remains the question of my father."

"I see," the King murmured. "Regarding the first matter: I thought we had reached an arrangement, a financial settlement?"

"Indeed we did. You will remember that when I left the airport I was in possession of an attaché case?"

"I do remember."

"I no longer have it," Mauricio explained.

"You mean you have lost the million and a half pounds?" the King cunningly asked.

"Every last cent of it."

"Then perhaps we could discuss how those funds could be reinstated?" the King offered.

"That is kind of you indeed. But first let's consider the more pressing question of my father, whom I have yet to 'see' as per our original arrangement. I mean can you tell me what happened at the airport, why Lord Embers was unable to fulfil his side of the bargain?"

"I'm afraid I really can't answer for Lord Embers," the King said with a measure of impatience, whether it was feigned or not it was difficult to tell. "When it comes to the breaking of understandings, it is a mistake to draw too many conclusions."

"Or make allowances?"

"With respect, that's not for me to judge."

"Hmmm," Mauricio mused. "Because I have to say I do now find our present situation rather confusing. You see a fortnight ago, when we first spoke on this matter, my feeling was that I *did* wish to 'see' my father, this man who was so free with his seed. Only now he has broken his word I find myself thinking perhaps I don't wish to after all! Except I'm torn: I simply don't know any more. On the one hand I may go through life forever wondering about him. On the other hand, well, what good can come of endless speculation? Answer me that."

"Only you will know the answer to that question, I'm afraid," the King pointed out.

"But I don't know the answer, that's the point. And the more I ponder the problem, the more confused I become, it seems."

"Then I don't see how we can proceed," the King frowned.

"Perhaps we should have the decision adjudicated?"

"By whom?"

"I tell you by whom," Mauricio declared, placing a

gold sovereign on the glass top between them. "How about by this?"

At the sight of the coin the King blanched. "How did you come by that?" he whispered.

"Being one of the coins in the velvet purse, I thought it might be interesting to hold one back as a souvenir."

"Did you?"

"So perhaps we could use this to establish whether I 'see' my father or not?"

"What about the money?" the King countered.

"I am thinking we could consider the matter of the money as a separate issue? Concentrating rather on this more fundamental question, blood being thicker than water, you understand."

"Very well."

"So in terms of this business of my father," Mauricio went on – and there was something of the look of a cat in his expression of concentrated stillness – "I'm going to call **HEADS** I insist on seeing him as per our previous arrangement, that is in a shopping mall or on an airport concourse. But if the coin lands **TAILS** then so be it: it was not meant that I should see him after all."

Here the King was seen to swallow and frown deeply. "Did you hear that, Big Ben?" he whispered.

"I did, Sir."

"And you heard it, too, PJ?" Mauricio asked.

"I heard **HEADS** you'll see your father and **TAILS** you'll not bother."

Mauricio then made a show of holding the gold

sovereign by its rim for all those present to inspect and be assured that there were, indeed, two faces.

"But I tell you what, rather than my tossing this coin, which might be seen to involve some kind of trickery, why don't we have an independent person spin it for us? Our friend here from south of the river, perhaps?" Mauricio suggested.

"Oh, I don't think that would do," the King objected.

"Or Big Ben?" Mauricio offered.

"I don't think he wishes to officiate, either," the King objected a second time.

"Or your good self, Sir?"

"Oh no, I could not be party to that. You see, I no longer wager."

"But you wouldn't be wagering. It is I who am consulting the oracle, not your good self. You would only be acting as steward."

And so it was that the King took the sovereign from between Mauricio's fingers. At first it seemed he might hand it straight back. Then he was seen by all to be carefully turning it over on the palm of his hand, as if unconsciously checking the two faces for himself.

"Very well," he said at last. "As you rightly point out it is not I who am wagering, only officiating."

"That's well put, Sir."

"So are you ready?"

"Never more ready! **HEADS** I insist on seeing my father. **TAILS** it's not meant to be."

As was the King's way, he did not try to catch the coin in order to present it on the back of this hand, rather he let it fall to the ground, where it fell clear of the table and so in perfect view to all assembled.

TAILS.

"So there we have it. I shall not be seeing him after all," Mauricio shrugged, perfectly matter of fact. "Although if I'm honest I had rather imagined the coin would fall that way."

"But look here," the King couldn't help himself from stating. "I think Lord Embers does rather wish it that you 'see' him."

"He does?"

"More than that, in fact, sir. My understanding is that he would like you to look into his eyes and in that way for there to be some form of acknowledgement – on both your parts."

At this the man from the barrios was genuinely startled. "*Really*?" he whispered.

"That is my impression."

"You mean he wishes that we should be introduced? That he should take me by the hand? And then take me out to lunch?"

"I'm not certain about that," the King cautiously answered.

"Then how could our seeing one another be accomplished?"

"What about in a mirror?" the Sovereign suggested.

"In a mirror? Now I would never have thought of that! But how could we see one another in a mirror without seeing one another in the flesh?"

The King had given this some prior thought, too. In

fact the answer had occurred to him on the walk through Green Park.

"Perhaps you could both enter one of our staterooms at the palace, each of you by a different entrance. Then, in an interconnecting door, in other words in the doorway through which you pass from one room into another, we could place a mirror. You could then both stand either side of this doorway and see one another's reflection without seeing one another in the flesh."

"I don't know about that," Mauricio grimaced. "I mean, I can see any number of problems that might arise from such an arrangement. What would stop my father from breaking his word and rushing into the room in which I was standing, for instance?"

"Lord Embers is my godson and I can personally vouch for him," the King stated with a solemn nod of the head.

"You're suggesting we should toss on that, then? On whether we see one another's reflection in a mirror?" Mauricio asked.

"In principle, yes," the King answered.

"But haven't we already had the matter adjudicated? Wouldn't it be in rather bad taste to consult the oracle again and in so doing potentially overthrow its previous directive?"

"Not with the introduction of a financial element," was the King's answer.

"By that you mean what?"

"By that I mean this: you have had the misfortune of losing one and a half million sterling in Scotland, am I right?" the King said, careful not to catch the other's eye.

"Why don't I offer to reinstate that sum, which could act as a banker, a guarantee of sorts. The condition being that I have the right at a cost of, say, doubling the stake, to purchase a retrial in the decision making."

"I don't follow you."

"I'm suggesting that if the coin determines you make your way to the airport then you do so with three million instead of a million and a half. But if it directs that you stay in London to see your father, then you have the assurance of this sum I am pledging to replace, the million and a half, I mean."

"You mean that on the toss of this coin I could be making my way to the airport with three million instead of a million and a half?"

"That is exactly what I propose."

"You have the sovereign, Sir."

This time there was a more excited tone in the King's voice. "To be clear what do you call?"

"I call **HEADS** for this business of the mirror and one and a half million pounds . . . and **TAILS** I leave for the airport forthwith with the three million net."

The King was almost too keen to toss the coin, and had to hold himself back a moment for the sake of propriety. Finally he cleared his throat and spun it into the air.

TAILS.

"So it *is* to be the airport," Mauricio sighed. "Of course I am delighted to have won the call, but in some ways it is so disappointing."

"Look here. My impression is Lord Embers does *need*

to see you, in the sense that you see him back," the King interrupted the other. "Would you consider wagering again on the matter?"

"Again on the matter?"

"By which I mean doubling up on the three million."

"Ready when you are!"

For an instant the King was seen to falter and to shudder slightly, as if someone had walked over his grave. It was only fleeting – long enough, though, for Big Ben to try and intervene.

"Your Highness," he whispered.

"What is it, Big Ben?"

"Do you really think this is wise?"

"Don't you see, I'm gaming," the other replied, turning to face Mauricio with the gold sovereign at the ready. "So: what's your call?" he asked the man from the barrios.

"Exactly the same as before," the other sang. "It's **HEADS** I stay and **TAILS** I go."

• • •

The King returned to the palace ashen. In fact unable to make the journey back across the park on foot, he had had to send for a car.

Cal and Kai heard the Sovereign out without any show of shock. They were perfectly familiar, after all, with the nature of the affliction of gambling – "the disease" as it was known in their fraternity – how once a session of gaming has started how difficult it can be to stop.

"All my life I have wagered but I had no idea it could

be like this, no idea at all," the King finished. "Doubtless it was foolhardy to seek guidance from the coins in matters where decisions were difficult to come by. And frivolous to fill the day with distractions, by which I mean a simple bet on a game of billiards or a punt on one of my yearlings: it only seemed to invest time with an interest which the day might otherwise have lacked. But to have wagered so fast and on a matter of such delicacy and significance, this is indeed a shock to me. I can only offer everyone my most sincere apologies."

"What exactly have you lost?"

"A very great deal of money," the King didn't answer the question. "How the coins fell like that I will never know."

"Perhaps there was chicanery?" the Californian suggested.

"I think not. I even insisted we use one of my own sovereigns," the King shook his head, producing the very coin used in the decision-making.

Both Kai and Cal turned the sovereign over in their fingers.

"But there *must* have been some ruse?" Lord Embers sought to persuade his godfather.

"Not necessarily. Fate can be like that," the taxi driver said with a rueful smile.

"I can now endorse that," the King agreed. "Again and again the man from the barrios kept backing TAILS and it came up TAILS. And when suddenly, for no apparent reason, no reason whatsoever, he called HEADS – well then, there I was: a loser again."

"So what was at stake?"

"Robert, I have lost a fortune. Not my kingdom, but some of the palaces."

"You haven't!"

"This one included: the ground under our very feet, in other words."

"But you couldn't let him have it, he's no more than a criminal," Lord Embers cried.

There was a moment of reflection as each in the party assessed the use of this word, spoken by a father of his son. Indeed Lord Embers himself may have thought he had gone too far, as it was seen that he had blushed.

"I always settle my debts," the King said at last.

"But what will your subjects say on the matter?" Kai countered.

"What indeed? It may well be that I shall have to abdicate."

Now a real silence fell on the assembled company.

"Of course, it may be it was coins instructing me to do this," the King wondered aloud. "Look at the state of these rooms, for instance. Tired and threadbare, they haven't seen improvements since the days of my parents' tenure."

"But Your Highness," Big Ben stepped forward, "you are much loved by your subjects. You are held in steadfast esteem."

"Will they still think that when another's colours are flying from the flagstaff? I rather think not! I am no more than a figurehead."

"But, Sir!"

"No Sirs about it, Big Ben. But the worst of it is I have further implicated you, Robert," the King said, turning again to his godson.

"How?"

"The man from the barrios has given me one last chance to redeem myself."

"Go on?"

"He is prepared to go double or quits on one last submission to chance."

"What submission?"

"You told me yesterday in Scotland that you wished to look into your son's eyes and that he should look back at you, and in that expression there should be some form of acknowledgement?"

"Yes?"

"He is prepared to gamble on that eventuality."

"What do you mean?"

"I mean that he proposes that the fall of the coin should decide the matter. That if it declares you should 'see' one another, then he is prepared to forfeit all that he has won in *The Ritz* this morning. In which case he would return to his home country with the original contents of the attaché case, which I have promised to make good."

"And if we don't wager?"

"Then I must honour my debts."

Lord Embers was on the verge of tears now. "The thought of us seeing one another terrifies me, though," he managed to make himself heard.

"Which is why I suggested to the man from the barrios that you don't see one another in the flesh."

"Then how?"

"Instead I have negotiated that you view one another in a mirror."

And here the King outlined his plan of placing a mirror in a doorway of two adjoining rooms. And how each man, in effect standing next to one another only separated by a wall, would be able to see the other's reflection and no more.

"I put it to him we set everything up here at the palace, but he's insisted the final wager should take place on neutral ground."

"Where?" Lord Embers asked his godfather.

"There was a fellow there with a piece of his ear missing. As far as I can make out it was he who suggested a public house in Chiswick, which has the advantage of being on the way to Heathrow Airport."

"A pub?"

"It's called *The Moriarty*. Apparently it suits our purposes perfectly, having both a Bar and a Lounge, the two separated by a partition but serviced by a common counter at the back of which is hung one long, continuous mirror."

"And the fall of the coin will decide whether I see my son in this mirror? I'm afraid I can't go along with this," Lord Embers was sure.

"Then I must settle my debts. And the sooner the better," the King said, turning to his valet. "Big Ben, go and phone for Askley and tell him to come immediately, and to bring as many assistants as needs be to process the clerical work."

"Wait!" Lord Embers stood.

The assembled party appeared to be shocked by the force of Lord Embers' intervention, forceful as it was.

"You have put me in an impossible position," the young Lord began. "If I don't agree to go along with this plan of yours then who knows your own destiny, Sir, and that of the great public, which holds you in such esteem. But if I *do* go along with it and the coin referees that I see my son, then perhaps, contrary to my own conscious reservations, I do wish some form of acknowledgment from the man I brought into this world after all."

"So?" the King frowned.

"I propose *I* consult the coin."

"*You* consult the coin?"

"**HEADS** we go to *The Moriarty*. **TAILS** we don't."

"But you can't toss a coin on a matter of such delicacy," the King was heard to say.

Silence.

"Can he?" the King asked Kai and then Cal.

"I can only say that I wouldn't," the taxi driver answered.

"Nor me," Kai agreed.

"So then what *would* you do?" the King pressed the former.

"I would take time to understand my intentions, Sir. And in so doing ask for assistance."

"From whom?"

"From God."

"From *God*?" the King repeated, aghast. "What has God to do with this?"

"The affliction of gambling is a symptom of a spiritual malaise, Your Highness. With respect, Sir, it has everything to do with God."

"Well, I, for one, don't believe in God. Not under these circumstances, anyway," Lord Embers declared, and taking a step back, he tossed the coin, which fell spinning to the ground . . . landing **HEADS.**

• • •

And so that evening a party of five was seen to set out from the palace. The weather had taken a turn for the worse. Perhaps there was even the first scent of autumn in the air, as on the pavements there was evidence of fallen leaves. In anticipation of the rain that was forecasted, all were wearing mackintoshes, some of these of a style from years gone by: beige and double-breasted with heavy lapels and thick belts.

In fact the winds had been so strong that warnings of possible flooding had been issued, something that only threatened in the event of a high tide coinciding with a surge storm. Any real problems would be downstream of Chiswick, the Met Office had made clear. Nevertheless Big Ben was beholden to warn his Sovereign of the potential danger.

"No, Big Ben, we are going to Chiswick, whether it's under water or not," the King said, waving the other's objections aside.

• • •

Presently they arrived at their destination, a quiet pub set back from the main thoroughfare. There had been much negotiation between the parties as to how this meeting should be orchestrated. The main considerations being that the two main protagonists should never catch sight of one another in the flesh and that the pub should be closed to regulars and anyone else in need of refreshment.

The publican, well known to PJ, had been most helpful in both regards. In addressing the first concern he had concealed the mirror behind a blanket pending the outcome of this last submission to chance. This would enable both parties to assemble either side of the partition in readiness for the last wager. All this had been done with the help of PJ and Big Ben, who were acting as quasi seconds. They had even tossed a coin to determine which party would take the Public Bar and which the Lounge.

"This way, Sir," Big Ben said, guiding the Sovereign into the latter.

"Well, at least we have won that bet, if we don't win any others," the King was heard to say with a dry laugh.

The Prendice brothers, who were charged with handling the cash and promissory notes, had been following in a silver Audi. Once the King was settled in the Lounge, two cases were brought in and placed on a table prepared especially to accommodate them. Finally Lord Embers entered and took his place. Visibly pale and hollow-cheeked, it seemed he was unable to take his eyes from the mirror, concealed as it was by a grey, utilitarian blanket, in a way perhaps a man would view the scaffold prepared for his execution. At the sight of his godson suffering so, the King was understandably contrite.

"I simply don't know what to say," he kept repeating to his godson.

"It will be as the coin decides, Sir," Lord Embers tried to reassure the other. "In many ways I am happy to have the decision taken out of my hands."

"Whether that is a worthy sentiment, I am not in a position to judge – but it is one with which I am familiar, nonetheless."

Just then a hush fell over the party, it being apparent that Mauricio and his representatives had entered the Public Bar and were readying themselves for what was to follow. Like hounds drawing a covert, the King and his party twisted their heads to hear the better, although all they could really discern was the sound of a door being opened and closed and the storm beyond it. Finally there came the sound of PJ clearing his throat.

"Are you there?" he called over the partition.

"We are," Big Ben replied.

"The Lord Embers is in position?"

"He is. And your man?"

"Nearly so."

"And what does that mean?"

"It means we need to see the money."

At this Ernest Prendice took the cases and placed them on the counter, directly behind the partition of panelled oak, which made them equally visible to both parties.

"Now open them," PJ was heard to say.

This was done.

"We are ready now," PJ then said.

But who was to toss the coin? That was the one matter that remained undecided. And here was the first time Mauricio spoke. And the first time his father had heard his son's voice since he had heard it in *The Weir Pool.*

"Let the King take charge of it, he did a good enough job in *The Ritz.*"

"But I don't want to," the King whispered to Big Ben. "Not after all the bad calls I've made already."

"Please officiate, Sir," Lord Embers begged his godfather.

"Robert, ask the American. Or the taxi driver."

The taxi driver would not agree, but he was determined that the American should take the role.

"I don't think so," Kai frowned.

"My friend, here is your chance to be free of this business once and for all. The story has come full circle and I believe that by officiating you will achieve closure."

"You really think so?"

"I know it to be the case."

"What's the delay?" came Mauricio's voice once again.

"No delay," Big Ben answered. "I shall be overseeing the stake and the mirror and it is the American who shall be throwing the coin."

"Come on, then, let's have it done."

At last Big Ben was ready, in front of him the cases of money, behind him the hanging blanket of coarse felt. The publican would like to have occupied his usual place, too, from which he served his customers, but was asked to step into the taproom behind. So all eyes were on Kai, who could see both parties, but whose expression betrayed nothing, only the solemnity of the occasion. Beyond that there was the sound of the storm, which had intensified considerably in the interim, the rain drumming on the roof so loudly it reminded Cal of his childhood home in the Caribbean.

"Before me I have two suitcases. In one the sum of one and a half million pounds. In the other twenty-four million pounds and promissory notes relating to securities," Big Ben summarized the position. "And behind me a mirror concealed at present by a blanket. If the coin lands **HEADS** you, Sir, take this case containing a greater sum of money and proceed directly to the airport, the cover remaining intact. **TAILS** and the mirror is revealed and it is the other case containing the lesser sum you take. Who will be your representative?" he asked of Mauricio first.

"The man from south of the river," was the answer.

"And yours?" Big Ben asked the King.

"The taxi driver," the Sovereign answered.

"Both of you move forward. Once you are in position I shall instruct the American to throw the coin."

"Wait!" ordered Mauricio.

At this all parties in the Lounge locked eyes. Was this the point at which the man from the barrios would make further demands? And, if so, what could they be?

"What is it?" Big Ben called out for clarification.

"I think on a matter of such importance it should be best of three throws."

"I agree, I think he's right," the King whispered to Lord Embers. "What do you say?"

"Yes, best of three," Lord Embers indicated to Big Ben.

"Very good," the valet said, stiffening to increase his height further. "The best of three it is. My friend, throw the coin."

So here Kai tossed the sovereign, caught it and slapped it down on the bar.

PJ was the first to determine the outcome. "**TAILS**," he announced to all and sundry.

A second time Kai threw the coin.

This time it was Cal who leaned over first. "**HEADS**," he confirmed.

Thus it transpired that a decision of such magnitude should be determined on the deciding coin. Not that Big Ben appeared in the least affected. "**TAILS** I remove blanket," he said, gesturing for the coin to be tossed. "**HEADS** it stays where it is."

This time when Kai had plucked the coin from its golden parabola, he didn't immediately remove his hand once he'd slapped it down on the counter. Rather he let the coin stay under his fingers a moment, until both seconds were in a position to read the result simultaneously. Then he pulled his hand away.

"**TAILS!**" shouted PJ.

"**TAILS** it is," Cal corroborated.

And so Big Ben gave the blanket one decent tug.

What Lord Embers saw first in his son's expression was one of surprise and shock, unpreparedness, perhaps, for this outcome. This lasted for a matter of seconds only, however, as then the man from the barrios was seen to begin to smile . . . and then to laugh. A deep belly laugh that brought crows' feet to his eyes and revealed a gold tooth in the place of one of his incisors.

At first Lord Embers was taken aback by this reaction, and a look of hurt automatically clouded his features. But then he, too, began to laugh. A dry titter at first, and then in increasing depth. Until, he, too, was rocking on his seat. The more he laughed the more it occurred to him how handsome and how "well" his son appeared. Lord Embers himself was a healthy-looking man, but there was something about Mauricio's reflection in the looking glass that seemed to exude vitality and vigour. He needed to embrace that strength, feel it in his fingers, to taste, savour and share it.

But when, apparently involuntarily, he stood and advanced, arms outstretched, towards the bar, the laughing stopped. Mauricio was seen to hold up one hand as if to say: "Halt!" With the other he gestured to PJ, who was standing by the door to the street, and who seemed to be holding a candle in his right hand.

"My son!" Lord Embers breathed.

"Come no further," the reflection of Mauricio commanded in the mirror.

"But, Mauricio . . ."

Then there was a thunder flash, an earsplitting crack of gunshot intensity, the concussion of which shook the glasses on their shelves and moved the ground beneath their feet.

Next the lights went out.

"They're trying to take the money, Your Highness," Ernest Prendice was heard to shout.

Indeed they were. It seemed in the darkness both Mauricio and PJ were wrestling with Big Ben. There was much sound of splintering glass and it being ground underfoot.

"I'm giving you fair warning, take your hands from that case," Mauricio demanded of the King's valet.

"This is crown property and be under no illusion: it shall be defended to the last."

At this, though, the King made a counter command. "I order you to hands off, Big Ben. You are to let the cases go."

"Can you repeat that, Sir?"

"I said you are to let the cases go. Let them take them."

• • •

And so it was that the man from the barrios was allowed to proceed to Heathrow Airport with his booty.

"We shall not pursue them," the King told everyone assembled once the lights had been restored and the smoke had thinned inside *The Moriarty*. In fact it was the publican to whom the King turned first. "I shall instruct my foreman of works to draw up a schedule of everything that has been damaged here. You shall not be out of pocket," he told this honest man.

"Thank you, Your Majesty."

The King then turned his attention to Lord Embers. "It would seem, Robert, that we have a resolution to our problems, finally. How do you feel?"

"I don't know, Sir."

"You must feel something?"

"If I do, Sir, I would have to say I feel oddly calm."

"Well, in fact so do I," the King said, clasping his godson by the hand.

"Mauricio, my son, he looked so incredibly healthy," Lord Embers tried to articulate.

"I agree, it's hard to think of a healthier-looking person."

"He does not need me."

"And you do not need him?"

"Not in the way you suggest, Sir."

"Then we can ask for no more."

"And you, Sir, how are you?"

"A little shaken perhaps, but champion," the King tried to laugh.

Epilogue

"Long Live The King!"

About a week later Kai was getting ready to return to the States, when he heard that the King had died peacefully in his sleep.

"**THE KING IS DEAD**," the radio kept repeating. "**LONG LIVE THE KING!**"

Being not far from the palace and having a few hours to spare before his flight, he thought he might make his way up The Mall. Soon he was walking in a dense crowd, a crowd so dense, in fact, that at times it was difficult for him to be certain his feet were touching the ground.

The area in front of the gates, as had become the norm on these sad occasions, was already flooded with floral tributes. The thousands upon thousands of bouquets, which seemed to glitter and glimmer in the morning sun, could have been a vast migration of silver-backed fish, all intent on reaching their common spawning ground.

"What happened?" Kai asked a young couple.

"All we know is that the flag is at half-mast," they mournfully replied.

But another person whom Kai asked did know the answer to that question: he had heard it from his brother-in-law who had a cousin in the Royal Household.

The King had slipped and fallen in the storm they had just had, apparently, and striking his head on a stone step he had received a fatal concussion. All through the night the doctors had fought to save him.

"Slipped and struck his head?" Kai repeated.

"In that storm we just had," the stranger seemed keen to impress.

• • •

In fact the crowds were so dense Kai was over an hour late in returning to his hotel to meet Cal.

"We shall have to look sharp if we are to make the airport in time," the cabbie said, placing his friend's luggage next to the driver's seat. "But don't worry, I've an idea of how we can beat the traffic."

It was strange to be sitting in the back of Cal's cab; strange, too, to be conversing over an intercom. And so before long the two men fell into silence. The day was clear, as clear as if seen through water. And to begin with they made good progress.

Only before long, on a residential street in North Acton, they found the way ahead blocked by a vehicle which had come to exchange an empty skip for a full one. The procedure was new to Kai, and he watched on with growing interest as the empty skip was first lowered on top of the full one; the two then lifted onto the lorry bed, allowing the empty skip to be separated from its mate and to be placed ready for use back on the curb.

"That's darned clever," he murmured.

"What's that, Kai?" Cal asked, sliding back the glass partition so that they could speak properly.

"The way they changed the dumpsters here."

"The skips, you mean?"

"I guess, if that's what you call them," the Californian nodded.

The driver of the wagon was now tying a tarpaulin over the full skip before driving off. Evidently the workers engaged on the site were familiar with this man, that or they welcomed the interruption to their work, as they sought to assist where they could in tying the ropes to the skip's lifting points.

"And so what will you do now?" Cal asked his friend. "When you get back to California, I mean?"

"We shall rebuild our damaged houses," Kai replied without the need to think. "We will go from one homestead to the next," he explained, "until, one by one, they are all done."

"Aren't you a little old for manual work?" Cal goaded his friend.

Kai lifted a hand to the light. "Perhaps, but I'll help in any way I can," he replied.

"I'm sure you will," Cal nodded, more serious now.

"In fact I'm looking forward to it. More than that: perhaps it was what I was born to do: work with my hands, I mean."

And he explained to Cal how, with the help of others in the community, his own house had been built all those years ago. How in learning and perfecting new skills he had had to employ a much closer focus, one that seemed to help render everything else in better definition. It was that age-old question, he supposed – one so often looked for – of the sense of satisfaction derived from a job well done.

"The gaming which was once an obsession for us – the trying to anticipate events, the play with fortune, the abnegation of responsibility – it was missing the point, don't you think?" he finished.

"I don't think anyone can have the last word on our condition," the cabbie laughed, pushing the taxi into gear and inching forwards into a now open road. "Least of all us."

• • •

In Scotland Nick Winter had heard the sad news, too. With the same refrain repeated, again and again: **"LONG LIVE THE KING! LONG LIVE THE KING!"**

Thinking he needed time to reflect, he went directly to the river. Yet he found the news he had heard meant almost nothing to him. And this in spite of the fact that overnight, it seemed, the great beech trees that overhung the Tweed had become invested with the first colours of autumn; that there was the unmistakable scent of change in the air.

Presently his charge for that day, a young woman from Michigan and a personal friend of Mr. Richardson's, arrived at the fishing hut. Immediately they set about equipping the boat with the tackle they would need for the day ahead. And before long they were making for the far bank, the oars twisting in rowlocks made silken by use, a ripple gently tapping at the bows.

There was something about this young woman, whose name was Miss McKnight and who had thick, auburn-coloured hair to her waist, which reminded Nick of someone, and he wondered if he might have taken her fishing before? This was not possible, he instinctively knew; yet the feeling was almost as strong – or as vague – as a déjà vu.

For most of the morning they fished in silence, until, finally, Miss McKnight laid down her rod, sighed and seemed to smile to herself.

"Tell me, Nick, do you ever dream?" she asked him.

"Sometimes," the ghillie answered her.

"Well, let me tell you I had the most extraordinary dream last night . . . only I can't remember even a single detail of it."

"Those are often the best ones," Nick said, the words so softly spoken he might as well have been speaking to himself.

Miss McKnight had heard him, however. "I take it you don't believe in dreams, then?" she asked him.

"It depends what you mean by believe?"

To which Miss McKnight would offer no explanation.

• • •

After lunch, which they had taken in Mr. Richardson's hut, Miss McKnight was fishing from the bank when, at last, she hooked a salmon.

"I'm in!" she shouted up to where Nick was watching from a seat in the bracken.

Immediately it was apparent that this fish, so fresh it can't have been in the river for more than a matter of hours, was indeed a fine specimen. At first it went deep, then boiled at the far bank, before jumping well clear of the water, its belly as curved as a scimitar. Nick was quick to join his charge at the water's edge. It was strange. Not once in forty years had he used these words, yet now he was repeating them over and over to himself, like a mantra:

"Don't let it get off, Freya. Don't let it get off!"

She didn't, and finally, at the conclusion of a well-fought contest, Nick was able to grasp the salmon by its tail and lay it on the riverbank.

"That's the most beautiful fish I've ever seen," Miss McKnight said, overwhelmed by the sense of occasion. "Quick, we must take a photo."

Carefully placing the salmon in Miss McKnight's arms, where she had taken up position with one knee on the Tweed's stony shoreline, Nick took a photograph of her with the camera he carried for this purpose. Again it was strange. Possibly it had something to do with the way he was squinting through the viewfinder, because just for a moment he saw the elfin-like figure of his dreams, her hair, as thick as a lion's mane reaching to her waist as she threw her triumphant head back, her neck twisted as she half-looked down into the camera.

These being the days of catch and release, there then followed the business of returning the fish to the river. With one hand beneath its gills, the other under its belly,

Nick supported the salmon's weight in the current. Being a strong fish it didn't take long to recover; and with one lazy wave of the tail it glided off sideways, its gravel-grey back, like the shadow of a cloud, quickly dissolving from view in the peaty water.

THE END

Acknowledgments

I would like to thank my friends Martin Wilkinson and Emma Windsor-Clive, in whose house this story took shape.